AT A KIL

Davy lunged to his kne about to take a bead when Sontag crashed out of the grass and slammed into him like a two-legged battering ram.

Bowled over, Davy held on to Liz. Once more he heaved onto one knee. Once more he slapped her to his shoulder. Too late, he saw a rifle stock arcing toward him. He brought up Liz to ward off the blow but instead Liz was knocked out of his hands.

Sontag closed in. He was a broad man with a barrel chest and a sawtooth scar on his left cheek. His dark eyes glittered with sadistic relish. Here was a man who enjoyed inflicting pain. Here was a killer, plain and simple.

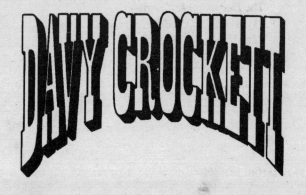

BLOOD RAGE
David Thompson

LEISURE BOOKS   NEW YORK CITY

To Judy, Joshua, and Shane.

A LEISURE BOOK®

October 1997

Published by

Dorchester Publishing Co., Inc.
276 Fifth Avenue
New York, NY 10001

ISBN 0-8439-4316-5

BLOOD RAGE

Chapter One

"St. Louis."

Flavius Harris rolled the words on the tip of his tongue. He savored them, as he would savor a mouthful of sweet honey. For long days now he had treasured them in his heart, as he would treasure a cache of sparkling gold.

A coon's age had gone by since Flavius had last set foot in a city. Normally, he shied from civilization, just like a cougar shied from human scent. But he had been adrift in the vast wilderness for so long that the notion of being among people again was downright appealing. Not to mention the thought of plopping himself down in a tavern and quaffing enough ale to drown an elk.

The gallivant into parts unknown had not been Flavius's brainchild. No, his best friend was to blame. Countless times Flavius had mentally kicked himself in the seat of his britches for being addlepated enough to tag along. He should have known better.

Flavius recollected all they had been through. The endless weeks of hard, blister-raising travel; their clashes with savage beasts, their deadly skirmishes with hostile Indians. And all for what? Just so his friend could see new sights, could roam new land.

That was the trouble with the Crockett clan. They were an energetic, restless lot. When they got a hankering to pack up their possibles and go for a trek, off they went. Woe to any idiot who tagged along. Flavius sighed once more.

"Are you homesick *again*?"

Flavius Harris glanced at the rugged Irishman seated in the bow of their canoe. He hesitated.

Davy Crockett was powerfully built, with a high forehead and piercing blue eyes. A coonskin cap crowned his thick brown hair. Buckskins clad his brawny body. Moccasins covered his feet. Slanted across his chest were a powder horn and an ammo pouch. On his left hip, in a sheath made by his second wife, Elizabeth, was a big butcher knife. On his right hip, wedged under his belt, was a tomahawk he had picked up during the Creek War.

Davy stopped paddling and squinted in the bright afternoon sun at his friend. He knew that poor Flavius was homesick, and that he was partly to blame. His incurable wanderlust had taken them a lot further than they had ever intended to go. Flavius had been pining for home for weeks.

"Well, are you?" Davy asked when his friend did not answer right away.

"What if I am? Can you blame me?" Flavius responded testily. "Any sane person would be."

"Don't get your dander up, pard. Another week or so and we'll reach New Orleans," Davy said. "From there, we'll cut straight overland to Tennessee. You'll be back in your cabin before you know it.''

"I'll believe that when we get there, and not before,'' Flavius declared.

Now it was Davy's turn to sigh as he resumed paddling. He knew that his friend was sore at him. But was it fair to hold him to account for events over which he had no control? After all, how was he to foresee the difficulties that had beset them?

Davy cast the matter from his mind. He was doing the best he could do. No one could rightfully ask more.

Their canoe wended southward along the mighty Mississippi River. On both sides the river rippled and gurgled. Virgin woodland hemmed the banks, rich green growth sprawling to the water's edge. Sparrows, robins, and other birds flitted gaily about. High overhead a hawk soared.

As Davy looked on, a large silvery fish leaped out of the river, then splashed down again in a shimmery spray.

Davy inhaled deeply. The wilderness always had the same effect on him. Invigorating. Intoxicating. More potent than the corn whiskey his kin brewed back in the hills.

This was the life! Davy mused. Roaming where he pleased. Seeing new sights every day. Having new experiences. Why couldn't his partner appreciate the beauty around them? Why wasn't Flavius more grateful for this once-in-a-lifetime chance to explore where few white men had ever gone?

A loud snort on the west bank caused Davy to look in that direction. A large black bear eyed them warily. It had come for a drink and been startled when their canoe swept into view.

At the sight of the bear, Flavius's mouth watered.

"What I wouldn't give for a thick, juicy slab of bear meat," he commented. Ever since they started down the river, they had made do with whatever was handy when they stopped for the night. Usually, that meant a meal of rabbit stew, or maybe fish, or even frogs. The last venison he had tasted was ten days ago.

"When we get to St. Louis, you can gorge yourself silly," Davy said.

"See if I don't," Flavius vowed. He made no bones of the fact that he liked to eat, more so than most folks. Food was his joy and his bane. He just never seemed to be able to stop. Where others were content with a helping or two, he'd treat himself to four or five. Or more. It explained why he was the chubbiest frontiersman alive. As well as the butt of more jokes than he could shake a stick at.

Davy glanced over a shoulder and smiled. "To make it up to you, I'm buying."

"You'll have to. My poke is about empty."

Truth to tell, so was Davy's. But the two bales of prime beaver plews resting in the middle of the canoe would replenish their purses. How they had come by the plews was a story in itself. One he did not care to reflect on at the moment.

"Know what else I think I'll do?" Flavius said. "I'm going to one of those places where you can rent a tub and get a shave for two bits, and soak for half a day."

Davy was genuinely surprised. "*You're* going to take a bath?"

"I know. I know. Twice a year is my usual rule." Flavius's sainted grandmother had warned him that too much bathing was bad for the health. It made a person sickly and turned them puny.

"More often wouldn't hurt," Davy remarked.

Flavius bent his nose to his left sleeve and sniffed. "I wouldn't be taking one at all if it wasn't for this damn fish smell."

Davy had to admit that the river did have a certain fishy odor about it. But after the first day, he had barely noticed.

"I can't stand this stink," Flavius said, scrunching his face in disgust. "Hell, my buckskins don't smell like buckskins anymore. If a painter got wind of me, he'd think I was a catfish."

Davy chuckled. "Too bad you can't shed your skin like a snake."

The plews caught Flavius's eye, and a germ of an idea was born. "Maybe I can. Maybe instead of washing, and risk coming down with a cold, I'll treat myself to a set of store-boughten buckskins."

"Why, you'd be the talk of the hills when we got back home," Davy said. Generally, the woodsmen of west Tennessee made do with clothes they fashioned themselves. Practically every woman was a skilled seamstress and could sew rings around a tree.

Flavius conjured an image of himself adorned in a sterling set of fancy buckskins with a rakish new beaver hat perched atop his round head. "The females would really be impressed, wouldn't they?"

"Especially your wife."

At the mention of Matilda, Flavius's glorious image shattered into a million pieces. So much for that bright idea. His wife would berate him without mercy for such a flagrant waste of money. Why, she might even resort to her rolling pin! It made him shudder. "On second thought, I suppose a bath won't kill me."

A bend appeared. Davy stuck to the middle of the river, where they were least likely to be taken by surprise by hostiles on either shore. The last thing he wanted was to tangle with another war party.

Thick foliage kept Davy from seeing much of what lay ahead until they were around the curve. The strip of forest to the west ended. High grass grew in its place, extending as far as the eye could see toward the distant horizon. It was a finger of prairieland, the grasses swaying in the breeze like so many slender dancers.

"Isn't it grand?" Davy said.

Flavius turned and blanched. He recognized that tone of voice. "Forget it. We're staying with the river."

"I wasn't thinking of going exploring."

"Sure you weren't. And the sun doesn't rise every morning, either."

Davy's mouth curled downward. It would be nice to venture westward, just for a few days. But without horses, exploring would be foolhardy. On foot they would be fair game for every grizzly or anything else that wandered by. Still, it wouldn't hurt to stop and rest. They had been on the go since before first light and now the sun was almost directly above them. A flat stretch of shoreline spurred Davy into steering the canoe toward it.

"What are you doing?" Flavius asked anxiously.

"Relax. It's noon, isn't it?"

Flavius squinted skyward, and grinned in relief. Usually they halted for half an hour or so about midday, then pushed on hard during the afternoon. Skillfully wielding his paddle, he helped bring their canoe broadside to the shore.

Davy hopped out, held the craft steady while Flavius joined him, and together they pulled it high enough out of the river to ensure it would not drift off.

Taking Liz, the rifle that he had named after Elizabeth,

Davy walked to an earthen mound a dozen yards away. From the top he enjoyed a clear vista of the prairie and the surrounding countryside.

All was tranquil. As Davy descended, he spied a set of peculiar ruts to his left. They led up out of the Mississippi and off across the grassland.

"What in tarnation are those?"

Flavius was rummaging through his possibles bag for the last of his pemmican. Straightening, he went over. "They look like wagon tracks to me."

Davy had dropped to one knee. "They are." He examined the closest rut, pinching some of the dirt between his fingers. "A big one, judging by the width. It went by a couple of hours ago." He rose and shielded his eyes from the glare. Scanning the prairie, he sought a telltale speck. There was none.

"What the devil would a wagon be doing way out here in the middle of nowhere?" Flavius wondered.

"Mighty strange," Davy agreed. The depth of the ruts told him the wagon had been heavily laden. Hoofprints showed that the team was made up of oxen. Different hoofprints revealed that a horse had been trailing a few yards behind, probably tied to the gate.

"Must be a trader heading out to do business with the Indians," Flavius speculated.

It was the only explanation that made sense. But Davy had doubts. To his knowledge, no one had ever taken a wagon across the prairie before. Based on the stories told about 'the Great American Desert'—as the plains were called—to venture out there on horseback was dangerous enough. In a slow-moving wagon, it was certain suicide.

Davy roved the vicinity. He found where the wagon had lumbered up out of the river, found where it had stopped, possibly so the driver could inspect the wheels and axles.

Then, as Davy was about to go to the canoe, he spotted footprints, two sets, off to one side. Astonishment coursed through him when he recognized one of sets as being that of a grown woman and the other as that of a child. "My ears for a heel tap if it isn't a family."

"Can't be," Flavius said. No one in their right mind would take loved ones out into that nigh-limitless sea of grass. Yet when he inspected the footprints himself, he had to concur. "Some damned fool must have a death wish."

Davy discovered where the woman and the child had climbed down. After a spell, they had roamed northward, close to the water. Small depressions in the soil hinted that the child had picked up stones, most likely to cast into the river. Skipping them, he reckoned, just as Davy had often done as a boy.

Something about the child's footprints bothered him. He had to study them long and hard before the reason dawned. The right foot always left a more shallow impression than the left. "The sprout is limping," he announced.

Flavius had already lost interest. Sitting on a log, he took a hungry bite of pemmican. "The kid will be hurting a lot worse if they run into any of those Blackfeet or Pawnees we heard tell about."

"We're too far south for the Blackfeet," Davy said. Still, his friend had a point. What could the father be thinking to commit so stupid an act?

Flavius chewed lustily. Pemmican had always been a favorite of his, even more than jerky. "Whatever happens is out of our hands. Their fate's up to the Good Lord."

Davy ambled into the grass, eyes to the ground. The wagon had been moving at a snail's pace, the woman and child walking beside it. Hand in hand, apparently. As any mother and child would do.

"They must not know what's in store for them," Flavius concluded. Although how that could be, was beyond him. The uncharted land beyond the muddy Mississippi was on the tip of everyone's tongue of late.

As well it should be. Tales had filtered to the East about the Oregon Country, a verdant paradise with fertile land free for the taking. And of California, a golden realm where, rumor had it, the weather never turned cold, and where fruits and grains grew in abundance the year around.

"We should warn them," Davy proposed.

Flavius sat up. He had been afraid something like this would happen. Afraid the Irishman would concoct some harebrained excuse to go exploring. "No," he said flatly.

"They have a child with them."

"So? It's not our kid," Flavius forced himself to say. Like Davy, he had a soft spot for children. But he was not about to go traipsing off into the heart of darkness to save someone lacking the brains of a turnip. "It's not our responsibility."

"Isn't it?" Davy countered. "Aren't we supposed to do unto others as we would have them do unto us?"

Flavius was so annoyed, he nearly threw his pemmican to the ground. "That's a low blow, quoting Scripture," he retorted. Davy was well aware that Matilda breathed fire and brimstone, and some had rubbed off on Flavius. Just as Flavius was aware that Davy had little truck with formalized religion.

15

Davy faced westward. The wagon was out of sight, sure, but oxen did not move very fast. "By nightfall we could overtake them."

"What about the canoe? And the plews?" Flavius argued.

"We can hide both, easy enough."

"No, no, no," Flavius huffed, rising. "I absolutely refuse."

"Then you stay here and watch our stuff. I'll go after them and be back by morning."

The prospect of being left alone chilled Flavius more than anything else could. "Damn your bones," he complained. "You're always doing this to me."

"I'm only thinking of the child. We should turn these folks around before they get too far out."

Having made up his mind, Davy was not about to change it. The Crockett family motto had a lot to do with his attitude. At an early age, the family saying had been ingrained into him. "Always be sure you're right, then go ahead," his grandpa and pa had instructed him, over and over. It was a precept he had lived by his whole life through, an injunction that daily guided his steps.

Flavius wanted to scream. Just when things were looking rosy, *this* had to happen. "If we ever make it back to Tennessee alive, remind me to choke you to death."

"You can stay," Davy insisted. He did not see why Flavius was making such a fuss. Another twenty-four hours would not make much of a difference.

"Oh, sure. And be snake-bit with no one around to suck out the poison. Or maybe I'll be chomped on by a gator. Or be caught by hostiles. Or run into another crazy old coot like that lunatic who wanted to take our heads—"

"I'm truly sorry," Davy said, interrupting the litany.

16

Flavius had a knack for finding more things to complain about than most ten people.

"That's what rankles me the most," Flavius said. "At least if you weren't, I could bust you on the jaw and have a clean conscience."

Secreting the canoe and the beaver hides took no time at all. A convenient nook shielded by reeds and low limbs virtually guaranteed that the craft would be there when they returned.

Davy slung his possibles bag over his right shoulder, draped a water skin over his left, and tramped westward, walking between the ruts. It felt good to be getting some exercise. Ten to twelve hours in the canoe every day left him cramped and stiff by sunset.

Flavius followed, but not too closely. He was sulking, and he didn't care to speak to Crockett until the mood wore off.

For over an hour, Davy held to a brisk pace. The sooner they overtook the settlers, the sooner they could retrace their steps. Early on, he checked his rifle and the two flintlock pistols tucked under his belt on either side of the big metal buckle to verify that they were loaded.

The grass had been partially flattened by the wagon's passage. It rustled against Davy's legs as he walked, no matter how hard he tried to move silently. Human ears might not detect it, but the ears of a panther or another beast undoubtedly would.

Davy never relaxed, never let down his guard. Doing so had killed more frontiersmen than old age. It only took one mistake, and a man paid a fatal price. Frequently Davy would rise onto the tips of his toes to scour their immediate area.

They had gone less than a mile when wildlife appeared. A small herd of deer, four does and a large buck, spooked from concealment, bounded toward the river. Flavius automatically brought up his rifle but the grass closed around their bouncing white rumps before he could squeeze the trigger. "Figures," he grumbled.

Another hour went by. Flavius's feet became sore and he stopped now and again to rub them. Each time, Davy got a little further ahead of him.

By the middle of the afternoon, twenty-five yards separated them. Flavius dragged his heels, wishing Davy would halt for a bit. He plodded along with his chin bowed, as glum as a rainy day.

Suddenly the high grass to his right rustled noisily. Startled, Flavius spun and glimpsed a dark bulky form moving parallel with him. Wedging his rifle against his shoulder, he waited with bated breath for the creature to show itself. The next moment the grass swallowed the thing whole. The sounds ceased.

What was it? Flavius asked himself. Another black bear? More deer? Or something infinitely worse? Cautiously, he advanced, the rifle held steady.

Davy was thirty yards ahead, or better. Flavius opened his mouth to call out, then thought better of it. A shout might provoke the animal into attacking. He walked faster, so fast that he nearly tripped when his left foot snagged on a clump of grass.

As Flavius regained his balance, he caught another fleeting glimpse of something huge and dark off among the waving stems. His skin prickled with bumps.

Whatever it was, the thing was stalking them.

Flavius tried to lick his lips, but he had no spittle to spare. His mouth had become as dry as a desert. He trained his rifle on a patch of barely visible hide at the very moment it vanished. "Damn!"

Worry gnawed at him like termites at wood. Every

18

nerve aflame, Flavius commenced jogging. If only he could reach Davy! The beast might think twice about attacking two grown men.

Flavius tore his gaze from the grass long enough to see how much distance he had to cover. To his utter amazement, the Irishman was nowhere to be seen. Bewilderment brought him to a lurching stop. "Davy?" he whispered.

There was no answer.

A low, rumbling grunt brought Flavius around in a flash. The creature was closer. Had it already gotten hold of Davy? Terror welled up in Flavius, terror so intense and overpowering that he almost bolted in blind panic.

By a supreme effort of will, Flavius calmed himself. All was not lost. He had a rifle, two pistols, and a knife. And when he had to, he could run like a jackrabbit.

Slowly moving forward, Flavius sought Davy's tracks. Any clue that shed light on Davy's disappearance would do. But the grass acted as a cushion, a barrier, preventing the earth from showing many prints. He saw a smudge here, a heel crease there.

Flavius heard a thud and crouched. Had that been Davy's body? Another thud, a lot nearer, enabled him to pinpoint exactly where the creature was.

He peered down the rifle barrel, afraid his hands would shake when the moment of truth came. Flavius would readily admit that he wasn't the bravest of men. Neither was he a coward. If need be, he would fight for his life with all the desperation of any cornered critter.

In the grass, a vague shape materialized, the same enormous, dark monster. Rumbling again, the thing barreled toward him.

Chapter Two

It was a buffalo cow. She came to an abrupt halt not six feet from Flavius Harris. They stared at one another, Flavius hoping she would consider him harmless and go on her way. Then, beyond her, a calf appeared.

Flavius did not so much as twitch. Any movement might spark an attack. Even though it was a cow, she could be as deadly as her male counterparts, particularly if she perceived him as a threat to her offspring.

While not as big or as heavy as the bulls, cows grew to a height of five feet or more at the shoulder and could weigh in excess of a thousand pounds. With their dark brown shaggy coats, broad, massive heads, and humped shoulders, they reminded Flavius of those ancient Greek monsters, those Minotaurs and suchlike, his teacher had prattled on about back when he'd attended school for five years.

The cow snorted and pawed the ground. It was not a good sign. Flavius continued to hold himself, and his rifle, rock steady. At that range he could not miss. But a single shot often failed to bring buffalo down, and the cow would be on him before he could reload.

Again she snorted. She took a step toward him, her flanks rippling with muscle. Cocking her triangular head, she regarded him closely. Nostrils flared, she sniffed loudly.

Not all cows sported horns. Flavius considered it just his dumb luck that this one did. She took another half step but displayed no more hostility. Apparently, she had decided he was not dangerous.

Then the calf bleated. It probably just wanted its mother back at its side. But the cow misconstrued. Bellowing belligerently, she lowered her head, tore at the soil with her heavy hooves, and charged.

Flavius had a couple of seconds in which to react. When she lowered her head, he whirled and bolted, fleeing pell-mell into the high grass, heedless of the stems that lashed his hands and neck.

A thunderous snort heralded the cow's onslaught. Flavius shot a glance over his shoulder and squeaked like a mouse. The huge brute was hurtling toward him like a runaway steam engine.

He started to spin and bring up the rifle. Fortunately, his left foot snagged on something and he pitched onto his side. By a sheer fluke, the fall saved his life.

The cow was almost on top of him when he tripped. She had gained so much speed that she could not bring herself up short, although she did slash at him as she went by, narrowly missing his hip.

Flavius shoved to his feet and ran. Why did these things always happen to him? He made it a point to always be considerate toward others and never mistreated animals, yet it seemed as if every time he turned around, somebody or something was trying to kill him.

His intention was to put a little distance between him and the buffalo, then flatten and pray she couldn't sniff him out. Eventually she was bound to drift elsewhere.

Another bleat brought Flavius to a stupefied stop. The calf was right there in front of him. In his unthinking haste, he had run toward the blamed thing, not away from it.

One look sufficed to confirm that the cow was bearing down on him with blood lust in her smoldering eyes. She believed that he was after the calf, and no wrath on God's green earth matched that of a mother protecting her child. She would rip and rend him to bits and stomp what was left into the dirt.

Flavius had no other recourse. Snapping the rifle up, he took a bead on her broad head. It wouldn't kill her, not with the thick bone that shielded her brain, but it might stun her and slow her down long enough for him to get away.

"No!"

The shout startled Flavius so badly that his trigger finger tightened. The rifle boomed, belching lead and smoke, at the very instant that a strong arm looped around his waist and bore him to the ground. He saw the slug gouge into the soil in front of the buffalo.

Davy Crockett held his friend down as the cow pounded past them. He had heard the bellowing and snorting and rushed back to help. "Do as I do," he directed, and scrambled southward on his hands and knees.

Flavius complied. The Irishman had a flair for survival, for always instinctively knowing what to do in any given situation. Time and again Davy had saved their

22

hides when Flavius had been convinced they were going to give up the ghost.

Davy plowed through the grass, scuttling like an oversize crab. The drum of hoofbeats disclosed that the cow was looping around to come at them again. He glanced around, and couldn't believe his eyes.

The calf was following them! Tail bobbing, head high, it had playfully tagged along.

Seeing Davy's expression, Flavius looked back. His heart sank. "Shoo! Scat!" he hollered, but the calf just stood there staring at him with its moon-shaped trusting eyes. "Go, you little idiot!"

Out of the grass swept Nature incarnate. Clods of dirt flew every which way. Fragile stems bent and snapped as a thousand pounds of raw brute force tore through the ocean of grass like a living hurricane.

Davy threw himself at Flavius, caught his friend by the shirt, and propelled them both to the left, rolling over and over as the ground under them seemed to shake and the hammering of hoofs rocked his ears. A clod struck his temple. Another hit his shoulder.

In a twinkling, the cow had gone by. She had missed again, though not by much. Davy leaped erect. Trying to hide would be pointless. She would not rest until they were dead. Unless he had an inspiration, and mighty quick, his wanderlust was going to be the death of them. It was root hog or die.

Flavius had risen to his knees. He was bruised and outraged by the antics of the stupid calf, which now trotted meekly toward him as if they were the best of friends. "Let us be!" he shouted, pumping his arms to emphasis. The calf completely ignored him.

Thirty yards out, the cow had circled and was on a beeline for them again. Her horns glinted in the sunlight, her immense form moving with remarkable fluid agility for a creature her size.

"What do we do?" Flavius cried.

Davy's response was to shove Liz into Flavius's hands, then leap toward the calf. It halted, enabling him to bend and slip both arms under its belly. Another moment, and Davy had hoisted the animal into the air. Holding it in front of him, he faced the onrushing cow.

The calf bleated and struggled, its legs thrashing, but Davy was not about to put it down. He braced himself, prepared for the worst.

The cow kept on coming. She was snorting and grunting like a grizzly on a hot scent. When she was a mere ten yards out, she lifted her head. Another few yards, and she swerved in a tight arc that brought her to a point slightly behind them and to the right.

Davy pivoted, holding the calf where she could plainly see it. "Get behind me," he told Flavius.

"I can shoot her now. I have a clear shot at her heart."

"No. The calf wouldn't last a week without its mother. Just stand behind me so she can't get at you without going through it."

Flavius was too exasperated for words. Common sense dictated that they kill the cow before she killed them. But as always, Davy insisted on doing what was right. One day, Flavius mused, that outlook was going to get his friend in a heap of trouble.

The buffalo was tossing her head and digging furrows with her front hoofs. Beside herself with concern, she plainly yearned to tear into them. All that held her back were her maternal impulses.

"Back off real slow," Davy instructed softly. Rubbing the calf's belly, he suited action to words and carefully tread backward. The calf had calmed somewhat but it continued to voice plaintive bleats.

Flavius did not take his eyes off the cow. If she came at them again, it would be up to him to stop her. He had both rifles.

"There, there," Davy said soothingly. "We mean you no harm, momma. No need to raise such a fuss. Calm yourself. All we want is to go about our business in peace."

The tone, not the words, had an effect. The cow stopped taking out her spite on the earth and stared squarely at them.

"See?" Davy said. "We can get along if you'll control that nasty temper of yours. We're just passing through." All the while, his left palm stroked the calf, which was quieting.

After retreating another five yards, Davy gingerly set the animal down. He patted its head, then resumed backing off. The calf looked from them to its mother and back again. "Stay, little one," he coaxed.

The cow shambled forward, grunting.

Flavius started to bring up his rifle but Davy grasped the barrel. "You're making a mistake," Flavius warned.

Prancing merrily, the calf rejoined its mother. They touched noses, then the cow nudged it and the calf skipped off into the grass. In its wake trotted its enormous guardian angel, tail curled high.

Only when the thud of hooves dwindled did Flavius breathe easily again. "That chuckleheaded shorthorn about done us in," he said, the tension draining from him like water from a sieve. He had always rated cows and their kin as being next to brainless, but this incident took the cake.

Davy claimed Liz, brushed the dust from the barrel,

and grinned wryly. "It's our day for youngsters, reckon."

"How's that?" Flavius said, and remembered th tracks of the child. "Oh. I plumb forgot." The encounte impressed him in a new vein. "Maybe this was an omen We should light a shuck for the Mississippi while we'r still in one piece."

"After we talk to the folks in the wagon," Davy per sisted. Bending his steps northward, he found the ru and hiked to the west. He hummed quietly, the clas with the cow all but forgotten. To him, it was just routine incident in a routine day. Compared to som scrapes he had been in, this latest was of no conse quence.

Flavius did not fall behind. He had learned his lessor But he did pout, convinced they were making a monu mental mistake.

The prairie rippled around them, the buzz of insects constant drone. Based on the oxen prints, Davy calcu lated that the wagon was an hour ahead, if that.

A break in the grass drew their interest. On the lef was a saucer-shaped depression some ten feet in diam eter. The exposed earth was hard packed and reeked o urine.

"A wallow," Flavius stated the obvious. It added t his worries, since there must be more buffalo in the gen eral vicinity. Wallows were made by buffalo rolling and rubbing the ground to form a dust bath. Bulls would the urinate in the dirt and roll in the mud. It helped rid them of bothersome insects and relieved chronic itching.

"An old wallow," Davy amended.

Another appeared on the right. Then several more scattered about. Dried buffalo droppings were added proof a herd had traveled through the region recently.

Davy guessed that the cow and her calf were stragglers. He was surprised that the herd had ventured so far to the southeast of their customary haunts, but it was not unheard of for them to travel clear to the Mississippi on occasion.

Without warning, the ground slanted downward. Davy found himself on the rim of a gigantic basin, a bowl worn by erosion over the course of many years. It had to be ten acres across and was dotted with more wallows. But what interested him the most was the object at rest near the center of the bowl.

"The wagon!" Flavius exclaimed, elated that they had caught up to it sooner than expected.

The oxen stood docilely in the hot sun, heads low. Tied to the back was a bay horse. It had heard Flavius and pricked its ears. But of the occupants, there was nary a trace.

Flavius scratched his head. "Where are the people?"

"They must be close by," Davy predicted. It would be the height of folly to leave the wagon and team unattended. Cradling Liz, he descended the gradual incline.

"Give a holler," Flavius suggested.

"What if they're resting inside?" Davy replied. The wagon was a style new to him. It had a cloth cover fitted to a frame, like the big Conestogas built by Pennsylvania Germans, but this one was smaller than a Conestoga and had smaller wheels in front than at the rear. The tongue was extra long to accommodate the four-ox team. Wagon, canvas, and rigging had a new look to them. Whoever owned the outfit had purchased it not long ago.

"See the sprout anywhere?" Flavius asked. Kids were forever conspicuous because they couldn't sit still or keep quiet for more than five seconds.

"Not yet."

Davy surveyed the basin from end to end. No figures were in evidence. He could not understand why the driver had stopped until he saw the busted rear wheel. "Look at that," he said, pointing.

"They must have hit a hole," Flavius said.

"Or gone through a wallow."

"Only a greenhorn would be that silly."

They were near the wagon. Davy made for the loading gate and was raising an arm to rap on it when the muzzle of a rifle jutted over the upper edge, almost in his face.

"Not another step, mister."

Long ago Davy had learned never to dispute a man who held a gun on him. Going rigid, he mustered a friendly smile. "Hold on there. We're not your enemies."

"So you claim."

The speaker was young, if his voice was any gauge. And nervous. Which put Davy doubly at risk. Skittish sorts were more apt to pull the trigger at the least little provocation.

"Honest to goodness. We're from Tennessee. We were canoeing down the Mississippi when we came across your tracks."

"And you trailed us all the way from the river just to pass the time of day, I suppose?"

The man's sarcasm was thick enough to cut with a knife. Davy answered, "No. To be honest, we were worried about you and your family."

Flavius could not keep silent. It rankled him that the man was treating them as if they were scalawags when they only had his best interests at heart. "Bringing a family out here is a boneheaded stunt. You ought to fix your wheel and turn around, or before long you won't have a scalp left."

The owner of the wagon rose above the gate. Twenty-five, at most, he had boyish good looks and was as thin as a rail. Homespun clothes covered his lanky frame. "Boneheaded, am I?" he said.

"My partner didn't mean anything by that," Davy apologized. "He doesn't keep as tight a rein on his tongue as he should."

"Think I don't know what the two of you are up to?" snapped the young man. "Think I don't know who hired you to track us down?"

Flavius was fast losing his patience. After all they had gone through to help these people, he felt it was damned rude of the settler to be treating them as if they were pond scum. "Listen, you yack. No one *hired* us. No one could *pay* me to trek across this godforsaken prairie."

"So you claim." The young man wagged the rifle. "Back up. And no tricks. I won't hesitate to use this."

Davy saw no point in resisting, just yet. It was obvious a mistake had been made. He counted on explaining fully and setting their suspicious acquaintance at ease. "Don't do anything rash," he cautioned as he took a couple of strides backward.

The man eased over the gate and slid to the ground. Despite his exceptional leanness, he was handsome in a rough-hewn sort of way. Sandy hair was cropped short. His eyes were a striking green, his jaw firm and prominent. He leveled the rifle at them, and for the first time Davy realized that it had been cocked.

"You can lower that hammer, son. We don't want an accident."

The young man was not pacified. Glowering, he said harshly, "My name is Jonathan Hamlin, as if you didn't know. And I'm not your son. Heck. You're not much older than I am."

29

Flavius was on the verge of exploding. Shoulderin[g] past Davy, he jabbed a finger at Hamlin. "I've abou[t] had my fill of you, you talking broom handle—"

Hamlin cut Flavius short by pressing the muzzl[e] against his ample abdomen. "Another word out of you[r] blubber guts, and you'll have a new navel."

Davy was about to intervene when another figure ros[e] up out of the bed. Stunned, he beheld one of the mos[t] beautiful women he had ever seen. Golden hair frame[d] a face that would do justice to the finest marble statu[e] ever sculpted. Grey eyes devoid of fear appraised him[,] then Flavius, and fixed on Hamlin.

"Be civil, Jonathan. I don't think these men are wh[o] we suspected."

Another head blossomed beside the woman's blu[e] dress, a dainty head framed by coal-black hair. A girl o[f] ten or twelve bit her lower lip, then asked fearfully[,] "Aren't they going to hurt us, mommy? Aren't they th[e] bad ones?

Jonathan Hamlin gestured. "Get down, both of you[.] I'll do what has to be done."

"No," the woman said.

"Heather, please," Hamlin said. "Let me handle this[.] I'm not about to risk your lives on the off chance you'r[e] right."

"But you can't kill them in cold blood."

Flavius had been momentarily mesmerized by the vi[-] sion of loveliness in the wagon. Now he recoiled, saying[,] "What's all this nonsense about making wolf meat o[f] us? We're as harmless as a pair of little lambs, ma'am.[']

Hamlin elevated his rifle as if to bash Flavius in th[e] mouth. "Like blazes you are!" he snapped. "Admit it[,] Dugan sent you, didn't he? Either to murder me or tak[e] us back to St. Louis."

Davy had leaned Liz against his side. Holding his arms out, palms showing to demonstrate he was peaceful, he said, "We don't know any Dugan. All we wanted . . ." He paused, debating how to best phrase it. Should he come right out and say that only a jackass would take a family on out into the wasteland? That he had gone to all the trouble of finding them just to convince them to head back to civilization before they were turned into human pincushions?

"What's the matter, Tennessean?" Hamlin said. "Can't come up with a ready excuse?"

Flavius looked at Davy. "Can't you see that you'd be wasting your breath? Let this fool get himself and his wife and kid slaughtered. It's none of our affair."

Heather sat on the edge of the gate. The girl boosted herself into her mother's lap and clung to Heather as if in mortal dread. "I don't want to die, mommy. If these are the bad men, make them go away."

Hamlin brought the rifle stock to his shoulder. "I'll do better than that, Becky."

"No!" Heather practically screamed. "For the love of God, Jon. Not in front of my daughter."

"Not ever," Flavius was swift to interject. He yearned to get out of there while they still could. To tramp back to the Mississippi, climb into the canoe, and head downriver. He yearned to be shed of the wilderness, shed of the endless brushes with death, shed of the atmosphere of violence that afflicted everyone, including a typical family like the Hamlins.

Backing off, Flavius said, "Look, we're leaving now. You folks go on about your business. Sorry to have bothered you."

Davy started to follow. He had to admit that Flavius

31

had been right all along. They should have left well enough alone.

Jonathan Hamlin did not lower his gun. "Not another step, either of you. Put your rifles down and shed the rest of your hardware."

It was the proverbial straw that broke the camel's back. Flavius had taken all he was going to take. Flushed with resentment, he brought his own rifle up. Or tried to.

Hamlin's Kentucky blasted. Becky screeched, her mother clasping the child to her bosom as Flavius staggered, then gaped down at himself.

"He shot me! The jackass up and shot me!"

Appalled, Davy sprang to his friend's side and slipped an arm around Flavius's waist as his knees buckled. A spreading stain high on the front of Flavius's buckskin shirt marked the entry hole. Fury filled him, fury directed partly at Hamlin for the callous deed and partly at himself for dragging Flavius there against his will. He was as much to blame as Hamlin.

Dizziness assailed Flavius. He tried to straighten, but his legs were too weak. First the buffalo attack, now this, he thought. "It just ain't my day," he muttered.

Hamlin had reached behind him and produced a flintlock. "How about you, mister?" he asked Davy. "Care to test my mettle too? You didn't expect it to be this hard, did you? I'll make you earn every cent of Dugan's blood money." So saying, he cocked the pistol and pointed it at Davy's head.

Chapter Three

Davy Crockett stared eternity in the face. Hamlin was on the verge of firing. He saw Hamlin's jaw muscles tighten, saw his trigger finger begin to squeeze. Another split second, and a lead ball would core his skull. The gallivant had ended as Flavius always dreaded. Elizabeth was left a widow, with six mouths to feed. Guilt flashed through him, guilt and regret.

It was then that a shapely slender hand swooped down from above. It gripped the pistol, and a finger slid between the hammer and the pan.

"There will be no killing, Jon."

Hamlin glanced up at Heather in baffled irritation. "What's gotten into you? Dugan won't rest until I'm worm food. And the fate he has in store for you is worse."

Eloquent mute appeal was mirrored in the woman's lovely eyes. "Please," she said, simply and softly.

Davy doubted there was a man on the planet who

would have been able to refuse her. Hamlin certainly couldn't. Bristling with suppressed anger, he nodded curtly and lowered the pistol to his waist.

"All right. If that's what you want. But you're making a mistake. We have to fight fire with fire, or our life together will end before it's barely begun."

"We can't stoop to their level," Heather said. "We're human beings, not animals."

Davy listened while examining Flavius. His friend was pale and weak, but more from shock than the severity of the wound. The ball had caught him in the fleshy part of the chest just under the shoulder, glanced off the rib cage, and exited without penetrating a vital organ or severing a major artery. "You'll live," he pronounced.

Flavius swallowed. His head would not stop spinning and he hurt like the devil. He attempted to stand, saying, "Help me up. I'm weak as a kitten."

"Be sensible," Davy said, and lowered Flavius onto his back. To Hamlin and the woman, he said, "You've made a terrible mistake. But at least you won't have my partner's life on your conscience. Give me some water and a cloth so I can tend his wound."

Jonathan Hamlin warily circled, then squatted to snatch one of Davy's own pistols off the ground. "You've got it backwards, mister. We tell *you* what to do, not the other way around." He wagged both guns. "Now get up."

Davy stayed right where he was. "Be reasonable. My friend is badly hurt."

"It's his own fault. He shouldn't have made the fool play he did."

The wagon creaked. Heather was climbing down. The

little girl followed suit, gluing herself to her mother's side.

"I'll lend a hand," Heather offered. Going to a barrel attached to the side of the wagon, she opened it, plucked a dipper out, and brought it over brimming with water.

Hamlin fidgeted. "You beat all, you know that? Why should you care about them? They're liars and killers, aren't they?"

Heather stared at Davy, her features inscrutable. "I'm not so sure. Deep down I have an awful feeling that they're telling the truth."

Jonathan snorted. "And cows can fly."

Bending, Heather gave the dipper to Davy, who in turn tilted it to Flavius's lips. "Here."

"What are your names?" Heather inquired.

"Davy Crockett, ma'am, at your service. And this gent your husband shot is Flavius Harris. We're backwoodsmen, on our way home after taking a tour of the country just to see what we could see." Over the years quite a few people had told Davy that he could be a regular charmer when he was of a mind to be, and he poured on the charm now to win the woman over. Showing more teeth than a cornered coon, he added, "Our wives will likely brain us when we get back for being gone so long. And the kids will all expect presents."

Heather straightened. "You have a wife and children?"

"She's my second wife, actually. My first—bless her memory—went to her reward much too young." Davy had to stop. A lump had formed in his throat. He had loved Polly with an affection as deep as the ocean, and her passing had affected him worse than any other.

Davy forced himself to go on. "Cruel fate entered our humble cabin and ripped from our children a devoted mother and from me a tender and caring wife.''

Heather blinked, then put a hand to her bosom. ''I'm truly sorry.''

Davy coughed. ''Young love is always the sweetest love, and she was my first.'' He looked up. ''Don't get me wrong, though. I adore my new wife just as much. No man could ask for a finer life-mate.'' He gave her the empty dipper. ''More, please. And that cloth I mentioned.''

''Right away.''

As Heather hastened to the water barrel, Jonathan Hamlin leaned toward Davy and said so only Davy could hear, ''I know what you're up to, you polecat. You're trying to win her over so she'll make me let you go. But it won't work. I love her and Becky too much. I'll do what has to be done with or without her consent.''

Davy frowned. ''You're as hardheaded as an old sour boar, you know that? If we had intended to harm you, why did we march right up to your wagon with our guard down?'' He tapped his head. ''Think, mister. Use that noggin of yours for something other than an ear rack.''

Jonathan pondered for all of three seconds. ''It won't wash. You came waltzing in like you did to trick us, so we'd be easy pickings. But it didn't work. Dugan will have to send out more cutthroats.'' He gave a start, as if struck by a thought, and stood.

''Who the devil is this Dugan you keep talking about?''

Hamlin bobbed his head toward Heather, who was refilling the dipper. ''You know damn well who Dugan is. He's her father.''

Heather had overheard. ''My stepfather, to be exact,'' she said as she came toward them. ''My natural father

36

died when I was eight.'' Sorrow twisted her smooth complexion. "He was a wonderful man. Loving. Compassionate. I can remember the Sunday walks he would take me on, just the two of us, hand in hand in the woods. Oh, it was glorious.''

Flavius groaned. The water had helped him some. His dizziness was fading, but the pain had grown a lot worse, so much so that he could have sworn someone was hammering on his head with a metal stave. Fingers pried at his buckskin shirt, hiking it higher. "Don't,'' he protested, suddenly remembering two females were present.

"Would you rather the wound get infected?'' Davy responded. Accepting the dipper, he trickled water onto the bleeding furrow the slug had dug.

At the contact, Flavius gasped. It felt as if an icy spear had been thrust into him. "What was that?''

"Water, you big baby,'' Davy chided.

Heather rose and whispered to Becky, who scooted into the wagon and was back in two shakes of a lamb's tail holding a washcloth, which her mother passed to Davy.

Jonathan Hamlin glared the whole time. He commenced pacing as Davy dressed the bullet hole, his fists clenched around the stocks of the pistols so tightly that his knuckles were white. Repeatedly, he scanned the rim of the basin, growing more agitated. At last he turned to Heather and stated, "We can't linger. These two might not be alone.''

"Jon, I—'' Heather started to reply.

A sharp motion by Hamlin silenced her. "I don't want to hear that you believe their cock-and-bull story,'' he said sternly.

Heather bowed her head and pivoted toward her daughter, who was a fascinated witness to the entire goings-on. Jonathan stepped closer, downcast, and draped an arm across her shoulders.

"I'm sorry to be so gruff. But I have your welfare to think of, and Becky's. As much as I'd like to take these men at their word, I dare not. Until they can prove otherwise, I must take it for granted that they're in your stepfather's employ."

"This whole mess is my fault," Heather said.

Jonathan recoiled as if she had slapped him. "Don't ever say that again," he said, and tenderly kissed her cheek. "Since when is being in love wrong? We could no more help what happened than we could stop the sun from rising every day."

Heather lifted eyes that glistened with moisture. "I know, beloved. Still . . ." She clasped Becky's hand and walked off.

Davy went to stand. He froze when Jonathan spun and extended the pair of flintlocks.

"Just hold it right there, mister, while I figure out what to do with you." Jonathan's brow knit. His gaze roved to the broken wheel and his mouth curved. "By golly, you'll be of some use, after all. Fix the wheel. You'll find everything you need in the wagon."

What else could Davy do? Hamlin had already proven that he would shoot at the least provocation. Davy unlatched the gate and swung it down.

The bed was filled to overflowing, crammed with belongings, everything from clothes to furniture. Tools filled a corner. Flour and other edibles were stacked in another. Blankets had been folded and piled on—of all things—a stove. Mixed among the effects was a butter churn, a rocking chair, and a washtub. Anything a family needed was there.

"Where are you folks bound?" Davy asked as he scrutinized the assortment.

Hamlin had shifted positions to cover him. "To the Oregon Country, as if it's any of your business."

Davy did not hide his amazement. "In a wagon?" Settlers bound for the new land always traveled by ship or steamboat. To his knowledge, no one had ever made the trip overland except for Lewis and Clark and a few traders with pack trains. "How will you get it over the Rockies? I hear they're so high, their peaks brush the clouds."

"We'll find a way," Jonathan said. Impatiently, he pointed at the corner where the tools were stacked. "Hustle, mister. I don't want your friends to catch up with us when we're exposed out in the open like this."

Years ago, back when he was too young to know any better and as cocky as a bantam rooster, Davy had run away from home rather than take a licking from his pa for an infraction at school. For two and a half years he had been on his own. He'd been a cattle drover. He'd ploughed fields. He'd done day labor for pennies. And, at one point, he had worked as a wagoner.

So Davy was an old hand at repairing busted wheels. First he set up the heavy jack made of iron-bound wood. It operated on a rack-and-pinion system. To operate it, he had to crank a handle that worked the pinion wheel, which raised the toothed iron rack. A pawl locked the wheel in place at the desired height.

Once the axle had been hiked high enough, Davy removed the wheel. It was standard, the rim made of curved pieces known as felloes that were pegged together at the ends. The spokes nestled into sockets in the felloes and in the thick hub. An iron band around the rim further helped to hold the whole thing together.

Wheels were designed in sections to make repair easier. In this case, all Davy had to do was replace a broken spoke and smooth the dented rim. The wheel was as good as new and back on the axle within half an hour.

Hamlin never once lowered the pistols. Heather and Becky observed without saying much.

Flavius lay where he had fallen, in too much agony to move. His whole body ached, his side worst of all. Once, when Hamlin came over to check on him, Flavius was half tempted to leap to his feet and bash the beanpole in the mouth. But he did not feel much like sitting up, let alone standing. He was content to merely glare.

After Davy replaced the tools and the jack, he knelt by Flavius to reinspect the wound. The bleeding had stopped. The skin around the furrow was grossly discolored, bruised by the impact of the heavy-caliber slug.

"What now, Jon?" Heather asked. "We let them go, right?"

Hamlin shook his head. "And have them lead their friends right to us? No. I've a better idea." Pausing, he smirked at the two Tennesseans. "We're taking them along."

Davy surged erect. "You must be joshing," he blurted, although he recognized full well that Hamlin was in earnest.

Heather was equally shocked. "Jon, no. Why in the world would you do such a thing?"

"Because you leave me no choice," Hamlin answered. "You won't let me do what's best. And I can't just release them. So they go with us, whether they want to or not."

"For how long?" Heather demanded.

Hamlin shrugged. "Two or three days should be long enough. It will take them another four or five to walk back to the river. By the time Dugan starts after us, we'll have too big a lead. He'll never catch us.''

Heather mulled the plan, then nodded. "All right. So long as they don't come to any more harm.''

Flavius could not believe what he was hearing. The day had gone from bad to worse to rotten beyond words. Another *week* out on the prairie? Another week longer to reach St. Louis? Another week more before he saw Matilda? He made a silent vow that if he ever stepped foot in the sovereign State of Tennessee again, he was never, ever leaving.

"Becky, bring that rope from up front,'' Jonathan said to the girl, who promptly dashed forward.

"Must you tie them?'' Heather said.

Hamlin clucked like a flustered hen. "You never cease to astound me. Do you want them to slit our throats in the middle of the night?''

Davy did not resist when he was instructed to place his hands behind his back so his wrists could be securely bound. He was prodded at gunpoint into the wagon and bidden to lay on his side against the bed wall. Flavius was placed across from him but was allowed to sit up.

Their weapons were collected and placed behind the driver's seat, within quick reach of Hamlin, who sat and unwound the reins from the brake.

Heather and Becky sat on blankets next to the gate, the girl hiding behind her mother and peeking out at Davy and Flavius now and then.

For the longest while no one spoke. Hamlin goaded the oxen with yells and the crack of his whip. He was wasting his breath. The team could only go so fast. Trying to spur them on was as futile as trying to spur turtles into a sprint.

Davy thought of home, of Elizabeth and their children, of the powerful hankering that had come over him months ago to explore parts unknown. He recalled his run-ins with the Chippewa, the Sioux, and the Thunderbird, and the many narrow scrapes he'd had.

Sometimes it seemed as if his life consisted of one escapade after another. The time he ran away, the Creek War, the mysterious malady that kept afflicting him, that fateful stave enterprise where he nearly drowned—he'd survived more than his share. Sooner or later, fortune would stop favoring him. Unless he mended his ways, his prospects of living to a ripe old age, as the saying went, were mighty slim.

Flavius was thinking of his cabin and his favorite chair. It always sat directly in front of the fireplace. How fond his memories were of the many evenings he had dozed in that chair after gorging on a venison supper! And what he wouldn't give to be sitting in his chair right at that moment, the fire crackling merrily, Matilda sewing at the kitchen table as she liked to do, humming happily.

Matilda. What a nag she could be. Yet she had her soft side as well. He would never have imagined he could miss her as much as he did. The first thing he would do when he got back was sweep her into his arms and give her a kiss the likes of which she would remember all her born days. She'd be shocked to her core. He chuckled in anticipation.

"What's so funny, mister?"

Flavius looked at the girl, who reminded him of a fawn ready to bolt if he so much as said, Boo! "I was thinking of my wife," he hedged.

"What's she like?" Becky asked.

"Matilda? She's a grizzly in a dress."

Becky laughed with the innocent abandon of those her

age. "You're awful! That's not nice to say about the lady you married."

"Ask my pard if you don't believe me," Flavius said.

The girl gazed at Davy from under her mother's arm. "Is that the gospel, mister?"

"Matilda is a feisty one," Davy conceded. "But she's a good woman. Just like your ma, I bet." As a child, he had learned that feeding sweet corn to a calf won over not only the calf, but often the mother cow as well. The same might work here. "She strikes me as being decent and kind."

"Oh, she is," Becky said brightly, and gave Heather a squeeze. "She's the best mother any girl ever had."

Heather's eyes narrowed. "Mr. Crockett, you wouldn't be salting the chick to catch the hen by any chance, would you?"

Davy laughed at her witty play on words. "To be perfectly honest, Mrs. Hamlin, the notion did occur to me."

"Dugan," Heather said.

"Ma'am?"

"My last name is Dugan, not Hamlin."

"But I thought . . ." Davy said, nodding at the front of the wagon.

"That we're legally wed? I'm afraid not. My stepfather wouldn't hear of it. And since he's a man of great influence, there wasn't a parson within two hundred miles who would do us justice."

Davy stared at the girl. Either Heather could read people's minds, or his countenance betrayed his train of thought.

"You're wondering about Rebecca?" the mother said, stroking her daughter's hair. "She's mine by a previous marriage. My husband died about five years ago. A boating accident.''

The sadness she radiated washed over Davy like spring rain. They shared a bond, then. They had each lost their first loves. Now they were each making new lives for themselves. Heather, however, was going to extremes. ''If you don't mind my prying, why are you traveling overland to the Oregon Country when you could book passage on a ship? It would be a heap safer.''

Heather leaned against the gate. ''Would that we could, Mr. Crockett. But my stepfather happens to own one of the largest shipping lines not only in St. Louis, but in the country. And he spread the word that under no circumstances was anyone to give Jon and me passage.''

''He's mean!'' Becky said with stunning vehemence for one so young. ''Mean, and evil as Satan!''

''Rebecca!'' Heather exclaimed.

''It's true!'' the girl insisted. ''He hit you, didn't he? And he wants to hurt Jon, doesn't he?''

Davy was curious as could be about the particulars, but at that juncture the bay let out with a strident whinny that brought their conversation to an end. Heather twisted, took one look, and shot toward the front of the front of the wagon as if her dress were aflame.

''Riders, Jon! Three of them.''

Hamlin slid to the edge of the seat and craned his neck to see behind them. ''Sure enough,'' he said bitterly. Turning, he glared at Davy. ''Friends of yours, Crockett?''

Davy did not comment. What good would it do? Hamlin would not accept a word he said. Sitting, he spied the trio descending the eastern slope of the basin.

"I told you," Jonathan reproached Heather. "You should have let me rub out these lying vultures when I had the chance." Hauling on the reins, he brought the wagon to a rattling halt, then ducked under the top. "Pray there aren't more," he gravely said while retrieving his rifle. Moving to the rear, he shooed Becky aside.

"Come to me," Heather said.

Davy had to lean to the right to see past Hamlin. The riders were coming on at a trot. Rifles glinted in the sunlight. In the middle rode a bearish man with a bristling beard. He sat hunched forward and bounced with every stride his dun took, a trait of a poor horseman.

Jonathan was reloading his rifle, his fingers flying. But he was as poor at it as the bearish man was at riding. Twice he nearly dropped the powder horn, and he spilled more black grains than he fed into the muzzle.

"Hurry, Jon," Becky urged fearfully.

Hamlin rammed a patch and ball down the barrel with the ramrod. He was apprehensive, but trying not to show it. Replacing the ramrod, he cocked the rifle, then trained it on the trio. By then they were within a hundreds yards of the wagon and had slowed to a walk.

"Shoot them!" Becky said.

"Hush!" Heather commanded, pulling the girl close and hunkering. "Stay down in case they open fire."

Davy saw the riders plainly now. None was dressed like a frontiersman. Coarse shirts and ordinary pants and boots were their attire. That, and small caps such as those Davy had seen worn by dockworkers on the wharves of Baltimore, back when he first ran away from home.

"That's far enough, Benchley!" Jonathan called out.

All three men drew rein. The bear in the center leaned

on his saddle horn and cocked his head. "You really didn't think you'd get away with it, did you, Hamlin? Give us the woman and the girl, or there'll be hell to pay."

Chapter Four

Davy Crockett did not hold Jonathan Hamlin in very high regard. Granted, the man was protecting the woman he loved, and her daughter. But that did not excuse some of the things Hamlin had done, and it certainly did not justify shooting Flavius. But Davy's estimation of the man rose a few notches when Hamlin stiffened in indignation and roared his reply to Benchley's demand.

"Never!"

The bear on horseback was unimpressed. "Don't make us come over there and get them. Mr. Dugan said you weren't to be harmed unless you raise a ruckus."

"Go back and tell your boss that the only way he'll get his hands on them again is over my dead body!"

Benchley said something to his two companions, both of whom nodded. "Be reasonable, Hamlin!" he bellowed. "I have no personal grudge against you. Why don't you step on out here so we can talk this over, man to man?"

Jonathan gnawed on his lower lip and glanced at Heather.

"Don't you dare," she said. "It's a ruse to put you in their gun sights."

Davy had a hunch she was right. Benchley did not strike him as the type who preferred to settle disputes with words. Flying lead and fists were more his style. "Listen to her, Hamlin. All they want is a clear shot."

Jonathan looked at him. "What do you care? Are you trying to win my favor so I'll release you?"

Davy clammed up. Some people just did not have the sense of a fence post.

Across the wagon, Flavius snickered. Would his friend never learn? Always trying to do the right thing had its drawbacks. Chief among them was that most of the human race didn't give a damn about doing right, and made a laughingstock of those who did.

Benchley's deep voice rumbled across the plain. "I'm not a patient man, Hamlin. Either send them out or come out yourself, or we'll start shooting." He paused. "You wouldn't want your sweetheart to catch a stray slug, would you?"

"He's bluffing!" Heather declared. "They won't dare risk hitting me. My stepfather would have them boiled alive."

Hamlin wavered. "I don't know . . ." he said.

Suddenly a shot rang out. A ball tore into the cloth cover above their heads and ripped out the far side. In pure reflex, Davy and everyone else ducked.

"That ought to show you we're serious!" Benchley shouted. "Now send them out."

Jonathan Hamlin rose, his cheeks scarlet with outrage. Leveling his rifle, he snapped off a shot. He should have aimed more carefully. Davy saw the cap on Benchley's head go flying. Benchley immediately reined to the right along with another man, while the third river rat reined to the left.

Hamlin began to reload and to talk, more to himself than to anyone else. "I knew it! I knew I should have shot Dugan before we ever left St. Louis. He has the money and influence to seek us out wherever we go. Killing him is the only way to settle this once and for all."

"Don't say that, Jon," Heather said. "There has to be a better way."

"Your stepfather got where he is by grinding anyone who opposed him under his boot heel. He thinks that he's God Almighty. Either do as he says, or suffer the consequences." Jonathan spilled black powder again. "Nothing would give him more pleasure than to spit on my grave."

"He's not *all* bad," Heather said. "I mean, he always treated me decently until my marriage. And even though he was against it, he gave Thomas a job on his steamboat line."

Hamlin stopped reloading to stare at her. "I can't believe that you're defending him! After all he's done to separate us! After *this*!" He waved at the prairie.

The riders were nowhere in sight, and the pounding hoofs had fallen silent. Davy figured that the trio had swung to either side of the wagon and dismounted. "They're on our blind sides now. They can sneak in close and pick you off."

Jonathan was capping the powder horn. "You think I don't know what they're up to? You think I'm an idiot?"

Flavius had to bite his tongue in order not to say what *he* thought. He was curled into a ball against the wall, in too much agony to lift a finger. The pain had reached a plateau and stopped growing worse. But any undue movement on his part might aggravate the wound again. He was content to lie there and let whatever happened, happen.

Again a rifle cracked on the prairie. This time the slug tore through the cloth cover about a foot above Davy's head and exited the same height above Flavius.

"That's another warning!" Benchley yelled. "And it's your last! Send Heather and the kid out, damn you!"

"Maybe we should," Jonathan said. "I couldn't bear it if either of you were hurt."

Heather slid across the pile of possessions to Hamlin, hauling Becky after her. "Don't listen to them, dearest. Please. We're in this together."

Davy twisted and thrust his arms toward them. "Untie me and I'll lend a hand."

Jonathan snorted. "Sure you will. With a ball in my back. No thanks."

"My word on it," Davy pledged. "Give me my rifle and I'll help you drive them off."

"Just shut up."

"Do it," Heather said.

Hamlin looked at her as if she were insane.

"I mean it," Heather pressed. "My intuition tells me that we can trust him." When Jonathan did not respond right away, she gripped his arms and shook him. "For God's sake, don't you start being as pigheaded as Dugan! I know you're worried about me. I know that you're doing what you believe is right for my sake. But you can carry it too far."

"Amen," Flavius threw in, but no one paid any attention to him.

"*Please*!" Heather pleaded.

Jonathan Hamlin was a study in acute misery. He

50

studied Davy, then the beauteous features of the woman he adored. His soul was torn. He balked. And at that exact second, when their lives hung in the balance, two more shots boomed and two slugs smashed into the bed of the wagon, low down this time, so low that one of them punched through the wood and narrowly missed Davy's leg.

"See?" Heather said. "Benchley will keep that up until one of us is hit."

It was the decisive factor. Hamlin gave her the rifle, drew a pocket knife, and dashed to Davy. As he clasped Davy's arms and poised the blade over the rope, he peered into Davy's eyes. "I pray I'm not making the worst mistake of my life. I love her, mister. Love her so much it hurts."

"You won't regret this," Davy promised. The instant the loops parted, he hurried to the pile of weapons and rearmed himself.

From outside another bellow. "We haven't got all day, Hamlin."

"He's closer," Davy guessed. Edging to the seat, he placed an eye to the opening. Somewhere in that sea of grass the river rats were lying low. Sniffing them out would take some doing.

Suddenly three shots cracked, two on the right, one on the left. Benchley and his cohorts had made the mistake of firing a concerted volley. They had all emptied their rifles at the same time.

Davy was up and out of the wagon in the blink of an eye. Sliding over the seat, he lowered his legs to the tongue. The oxen were not the least bit agitated by the gunfire. Like the great dumb beasts they were, they peacefully grazed, oblivious to the turmoil engulfing the wagon.

Hopping to the ground, Davy flattened and turned. On elbows and knees he crabbed under the bed to the front wheel on the right. A wall of grass met his gaze. He waited for one of the river rats to rise up and give him a target but the minutes dragged by and no one appeared.

"Hamlin! You still alive?"

Benchley's shout came from grass not fifty feet from where Davy was crouched. But try as he might, he could not locate the cutthroat.

"I'm here!" was Jonathan's reply.

"Are you ready to give in yet?"

It was Heather who answered. "If you want us, Rufus, you'll have to drag us out kicking and screaming."

"Awww, don't make it so hard on yourself, girlie," Benchley said. "I've never mistreated you, have I? Becky and you will be safe, I guarantee."

Through the planks that made up the floor of the bed wafted muted voices.

"Mr. Benchley bought me sweets once, mommy. He isn't so bad."

"Bad enough, Becky. Now shush."

"If only I could see them!" Jonathan complained.

"Where do you suppose Mr. Crockett got to?" Heather asked.

"He's probably out there with his good friend, Benchley."

Flavius interjected a remark. "Mister, I've met some boneheaded jackasses in my day, but you beat them all-hollow. My pard has more real grit in his little finger than you have in your whole blamed body. He'll give those thugs what-for. Mark my words."

Another volley rang out. Lead smacked into the bed, lower than ever. One shot passed underneath it and whizzed past Davy's shoulder. He had waited long enough. Throwing himself flat, he crawled toward the grass. Every foot of the way he prayed that the river rats were concentrating on the wagon to the exclusion of all else.

No shouts were raised. No shots were directed at him. Davy gained the grass and bore to the southeast. He parted the stems with Liz, careful not to make them rustle.

At the rear of the wagon, a rifle banged.

Ahead of Davy, someone uttered a guttural laugh.

"That quill pusher couldn't hit the broad side of a stable with a cannon," someone stated.

"You're forgetting he almost took my head off a while ago," Benchley snapped. "So keep yours down, Sontag, if you know what's good for you."

Davy had a fairly good idea of where the two men were. Benchley was to his left, perhaps thirty feet away. Sontag was straight ahead, and nearer. Davy angled to the right, going wide in order to approach Sontag from behind. A few more shots peppered the wagon, but no outcries followed them. Apparently, Flavius and the others were still unharmed.

The grass on his left rustled. Davy hugged the earth as a husky form materialized, moving briskly toward the wagon. It had to be Sontag, and the man's course would take him within a few steps of where Davy lay.

Davy twisted to bring Liz to bear. The thick grass should shield him, he reckoned, but once again fate intervened. Somehow or other, Sontag spotted him. A pistol cracked, the ball biting into the soil at his elbow.

Davy lunged to his knees, elevating Liz. He was about to take a bead when Sontag crashed out of the grass and rammed into him like a two-legged battering ram.

Bowled over, Davy held onto Liz. Once more he

heaved onto one knee. Once more he slapped her to his shoulder. Too late, he saw a rifle stock arcing toward him. He brought up Liz to ward off the blow but instead Liz was knocked out of his hands.

Sontag closed in. He was a broad man with a barrel chest and a sawtooth scar on his left cheek. His dark eyes glittered with sadistic relish. Here was a man who enjoyed inflicting pain. Here was a killer, plain and simple.

Again the stock swept at Davy. He dropped under it and rolled, deliberately churning toward Sontag's legs. He made contact, and down Sontag toppled. Davy whipped a punch that glanced off the river rat's temple.

Sontag had lost his rifle, so he resorted to grappling. A rough and tumble customer who had learned to fight in the no-holds-barred arena of the wharves, he fought as dirty as a politician. He kicked, he gouged, he even bit.

A fist caught Davy on the jaw and pinpoints of light pinwheeled in front of him. A boot slammed into his midsection with enough force to drive his stomach out through his spine. Dazed, in torment, Davy blocked several roundhouse punches, then threw a right cross that rocked Sontag.

"Bastard!" the riverman hissed. His fists were flesh-and-blood hammers, his knuckles the size of walnuts. The punishment he rained down on Davy would have crippled a lesser man. As it was, Davy was hard pressed to hold his own.

They traded a flurry, neither doing much damage. Davy was jarred by an uppercut. In retaliation, he landed a left cross. Sontag took him unawares by smashing into him and wrapping fingers as thick as knife hilts around his throat.

"You're mine, you son of a bitch!"

Davy leaped backward and swung at Sontag's wrists, but it was the same as pummeling iron. Sontag's thick fingernails dug in deeper, and Davy felt blood moisten his flesh. Davy jerked to either side, hitting Sontag's arms again and again.

"Puny feller, ain't you?" Sontag taunted.

No one had ever accused Davy of being a weakling before. Among the backwoodsmen of his home state, he had earned a reputation for strength and stamina that most men marveled at. Now he applied that strength, exerting every ounce of power in his steely sinews as he thrust his hands at Sontag, wrapped his own fingers around Sontag's bull neck, and squeezed.

The sneer on Sontag's craggy countenance became a frown as Davy's fingers sank deeper and deeper. Veins bulged on Sontag's face, and Davy imagined the same was true of his. Sontag began to puff and sputter. Davy squeezed harder. Sontag wrenched to either side. Davy squeezed harder.

Just when Davy thought the man would pass out, a knee slammed into his groin. Davy's strength evaporated like dew under a hot sun. He was shoved onto his back. A boot sank into his gut.

"For that, you suffer, boy."

Sontag reared over him, kicking in a frenzy. Davy absorbed several punishing blows, then found the energy to fling himself to the left and roll.

"No, you don't."

Sontag came after him, drawing a butcher knife. The blade glinted as Sontag raised it.

"I'm going to enjoy this."

Davy clawed at a flintlock, freed it as the knife streaked at his chest. He fired, the slug striking Sontag's

sternum and lifting the man clean off his feet. Sontag
flailed his arms like a windmill as he toppled. He struggled onto his elbows, sought to hike his arm to throw
the knife, and expired with a wolfish snarl of defiance
on his lips.

Off in the grass, footsteps thudded.

Davy pushed into a crouch, saw his rifle, and re-
claimed it. The footsteps had stopped. Benchley was too
smart to rush in blindly.

"Sontag?"

The whisper seemed to come from everywhere and
nowhere. Davy crept a step to one side. Where was he?
A hint of motion riveted his interest, but it was only
grass swaying in the wind. Taking a gamble, Davy circled, placing each foot with exquisite care. He had gone
a dozen yards when a holler arose across the way.

"Benchley? Sontag? Consarn it. What in blazes is
goin' on over there?"

To Davy's disappointment, Benchley did not answer.
It occurred to him that the riverman was probably doing
the same thing he was. A ruse was called for.

Davy searched the ground, but found only grass. Sliding his knife out, he pried at the topsoil, removing a
chunk the size of his palm.

Yet another yell broke the stillness. It came from the
wagon, and it was Becky. "Mr. Crockett! Mr. Crockett!
We need you!"

Davy tossed the chunk a score of feet to the north.
The racket it made when it came down should have
drawn Benchley's fire, but once again the wily cutthroat
had proven too savvy. Davy glanced toward the wagon,
worried by the anxiety in Becky's voice. What could
have happened? He dared not show himself, not with
Benchley and the other river rat ready to cut him down.

Nothing happened for the longest while. Davy had resigned himself to a battle of wills when hoofbeats drummed east of him. Leaping erect, he saw Benchley and the other killer galloping off, Benchley leading Sontag's mount. They reached the slope and clattered to the crest. On the rim, Benchley reined up and looked back. The gesture he flung at Davy was not Indian sign language.

Davy sped to the wagon. He was surprised to see Flavius Harris peering out, a rifle in hand. "They let you loose?"

"They needed someone who could shoot."

"What?" Davy said, hoisting himself as high as the loading gate. No explanation was needed once he saw inside. Sprawled on his back was Jonathan Hamlin, the left side of his head caked with fresh blood. Hovering over him was Heather, dabbing a cloth at a gash above his ear. In the background was Becky, trembling uncontrollably.

"He was hit during that last volley," Flavius said. "Another inch deeper and he'd be playing a harp right about now." He paused. "Or, more likely, shoveling coal."

Davy climbed in. "Fetch water," he told Becky, to take her mind off Hamlin's condition. Bending, he verified the wound was every bit as serious as Flavius claimed.

"It won't stop bleeding," Heather said anxiously.

"We need a fire," Davy said, and took it on himself to gather the necessary dry grass. He made a small pile. Too much smoke might advertise their presence to wandering bands of Indians. From his possibles bag he took a flint and steel.

Flavius covered his friend from the wagon. By rights,

he should be miserable, what with being shot and everything else that had taken place. But he was happier than he had been all day. Now that Hamlin would be laid up for a spell, Heather Dugan had to face facts and head back to civilization. She could not possibly make a go of it on her own.

Igniting the kindling was child's play. Davy fanned the tiny flames with his breath until they licked steadily at the grass. As he turned to the wagon, he almost bumped into Becky. "Sorry, little one. I didn't hear you sneak up on me."

"Will Jon live?" the girl asked bluntly.

"I reckon so," Davy said. "Once I'm through doctoring him." Davy nodded at the bay. "Does your ma have a butter knife somewhere in that mountain of belongings?"

"Sure. We have a dozen good ones that she only likes to use when we have company. And there are half a dozen old ones that she makes me use.

Davy smiled. "One of the old ones is just what I need. Would you bring it to me?"

She was gone in a swirl of hair and back again faster than a jackrabbit. "Here you go."

Davy pulled his left hand up into his sleeve and grasped the handle; the other end he extended into the flames. Gradually the metal changed colors, and when it was glowing good and red, he stood and strode to the wagon.

"What are you aiming to do?" Becky asked, dogging his heels.

"What has to be done," was all Davy would say. "Stay out here until we call you."

"Yes, sir."

"No matter what you hear," Davy stressed. Patting her head, he rejoined the mother, who glanced at the red tip of the butter knife and blanched.

"Must you?"

"It'll cauterize the wound and stop the bleeding." Davy positioned himself, his left hand flat against the unconscious man's temple. "Better hold his shoulders down. This will sting some."

That was the understatement of the century. Davy gently applied the knife. Flesh sizzled. An acrid stench filled the wagon.

Jonathan Hamlin stirred. Muttering, he tossed about, or tried to. Davy held his head in place, while Heather bore down with all her weight. Groaning, Hamlin opened his eyes. They were unfocused for a few seconds, until the pain registered. Then they widened and he feebly heaved upward, a scream tearing from his throat.

"How much longer?" Heather said.

Davy leaned lower. The odor of roasting flesh and singed hair reeked to high heaven. Little blood was visible. Slowly running the knife the full length of the gash, he did not relent until satisfied he had done a thorough job.

Hamlin gasped and wheezed, too weak to sit up.

"I'm so sorry, darling," Heather said, cradling his head in her lap. "Please forgive us." Jonathan tried to say something, but could not. She gripped his hand and stroked his fingers, aglow with joy that he would live. "Rest now. We'll take care of everything."

"Heather?" Hamlin croaked.

"Be still. Rufus is gone. Mr. Crockett drove them off. Everything is fine."

"No. It isn't."

"What do you mean?"

Jonathan's wide eyes roved the empty air overhead in blatant panic. "I can't *see*."

Chapter Five

Flavius Harris was as glum as a goat kept cooped up in a pen all day. Only, in his case, he had spent the last four hours cooped up in a bouncing wagon.

It was not bad enough that his wound acted up something terrible every time the bed was jarred by a deep rut. No, what made him especially miserable was the fact that the wagon was moving *away* from the Mississippi River instead of *toward* it.

For the umpteenth time Flavius vented his spleen by growling, "You've done gone and been out in the wilds too long, pard. Too much sun has fried your brain."

Davy Crockett was walking beside the left rear ox, whip in hand. It was the customary position for wagoners back East. That way, when oncoming traffic came along, the wagoner would guide his team to the right and be in an ideal position to keep an eye on the approaching vehicle.

Now, flicking the whip at one of the oxen that had a

habit of dragging its hoofs, Davy said, "It's on our shoulders to help these folks out. They won't last long if we don't."

"I have no argument with that," Flavius said. "What I object to is heading in the opposite direction of the one we should be going." Flavius stared ahead at the limitless expanse of rippling grass. "We're just asking for trouble."

Davy had about had his fill of his friend's complaints. "My ears for a heeltap if you aren't the grousingest gent alive." He cracked the whip again. "How many times do I have to explain the same thing?"

"You can explain it until you're blue in the face, and it still won't make no sense."

"Flavius, you beat all. You know that? Would you rather we'd headed straight on back and maybe ran into Benchley and his partner, lying in wait for us? Or maybe into Dugan and a dozen others, if Jonathan is right about there being a whole pack of coyotes scouring the countryside?"

"At least we'd be closer to the river," Flavius said, holding his ground. "If we had to, we could pile everyone in the canoe. Dugan would never catch us then."

"It's a mighty big 'if,' " Davy noted, and shook his head. "No, I reckon it's better this way. We'll make them think Jonathan and Heather are bound and determined to cross the prairie. Then we'll swing around and head for the Mississippi on a southerly track."

Flavius was cheered by the news. "No fooling? Why didn't you say so sooner?"

The fragrance of perfume and the swish of a dress announced Heather's presence. She leaned out, brushing against Flavius.

"Davy, Jon is asleep. I've done all I can for him, but it isn't much."

Flavius could not help noticing how the woman had taken to reporting to Davy every little thing that happened, and asking his opinion on the most trivial of matters. She treated him as if he were her brother. But then, that happened a lot. Folks naturally cottoned to the Irishman. Crockett had a knack for earning people's trust.

"Good," Davy said. "Let him rest as long as he can. We'll examine his eyes again after we stop for the night."

Heather rested a hand on Flavius's shoulder. "I can't thank you enough for what you're doing. And I can't apologize enough for how we mistreated you."

Flavius inwardly squirmed, bothered by the warm feel of Heather's hand and the heady scent of the perfume. He had always been awkward around the fairer sex. Even as a kid, whenever his female cousins came for a visit, he had fought shy of them except at meals and the like.

It wasn't that Flavius disliked women. Quite the contrary. His unease stemmed from an observation he had made when he was about twelve, an observation that subsequent experience had taught him was as right as rain.

Females were *strange*. Any man who thought they were normal either had no notion of what normal was, or had spent too much time attached to his mother's apron strings as a sprout.

All a man had to do was look at the facts. For starters, women weren't partial to logic, like men were. Their hearts ruled them, not their heads. They let their feelings guide how they acted. What made it worse was that their feelings seemed to change from day to day. Or minute to minute.

Take Matilda, for instance. One time she had gotten a hair to change around the furniture in their cabin. There wasn't that much of it, but what there was, Flavius had moved, at her command. They'd gotten done, and about an hour later she had come up to him and said they were going to change it around again. When he had asked why, she had said. "I just feel like it."

The table, the chairs, the butter churn, everything had been moved six or seven times over the course of the next week. He'd spend an hour arranging it just the way she wanted, only to be informed later that she 'felt' it wasn't quite right yet.

Was that *normal*?

Women were peculiar, and mysterious, and fascinating, all rolled into one. Some men couldn't get enough of them. Not Flavius. He'd rather deal with things he could understand.

Heather's voice brought an end to Flavius's reverie. "—don't know what we'll do if his blindness is permanent. We'd never reach Oregon Country."

"Don't fret about spilled milk until you've tipped the glass over," Davy said. "Doctors can do wonders nowadays. And a big city like St. Louis is bound to have one who knows a lot about eyes."

"We could never go back there," Heather said. "My stepfather would find out. He wouldn't permit me to leave again."

"You're a grown woman. What he wants doesn't count."

Heather grew wistful. "If only it were that simple. But you don't know my stepfather. What Alexander Dugan wants, Alexander Dugan gets."

"Can't you go to the law for protection?"

"What law? St. Louis doesn't have a police force yet, like New York or Philadelphia. Dugan is a law unto himself. Most of the politicians have their hands in his back pockets. And the few who don't are not about to make the mistake of antagonizing him."

Davy had known men like Dugan before. Rich, powerful, willful. They did as they damn well wanted, with no regard for the little people they trod on. To Dugan's ilk, common folk were so many sheep, to be fleeced at whim.

It was said that more and more of Dugan's kind were migrating to Washington, D.C. every year. That the hallowed halls of Congress were being taken over by the wealthy and their lawyers, by those who craved power for power's sake. If true, it spelled the death knell for the fledgling American republic. As the framers of the Constitution had warned, freedom thrived only when everyone had an equal say in government.

Davy had toyed with the notion of maybe one day running for Congress himself. He'd act as the voice of the common man, as a spokesman for those too timid to speak up for themselves. The backwoodsmen, the settlers, the farmers, they had a right to have their voices heard, and he had a set of lungs second to none.

Such idle musings occupied Crockett for a while. The afternoon was waning when he cast about for a place to stop for the night. Somewhere sheltered. Somewhere the wind would not chill them. Somewhere they could build a fire in safety.

There was only one problem. The unending plain was as flat and unbroken as a bed. No basins broke the monotony of grass, grass, grass. No welcome knolls or ridges offered a friendly haven.

"We'll have to make camp in the open," Davy announced.

Flavius didn't care where they stopped, just so long as they did, soon. His wound was throbbing, and he was hungry enough to eat one of the oxen raw.

Davy unhitched the team and tethered the slow-moving brutes and the bay close to the wagon in case Indians should try to steal off with them during the night. Aided by Becky, he had a small fire crackling in short order.

While they were gathering grass, he was reminded of something he had nearly forgotten. Becky's limp. Without letting on, he studied her and spied a long, twisted scar on the back of her left leg.

In the wagon, her limp had not been apparent. Oddly enough, when she moved quickly, as when she had been running earlier, it was less pronounced than when she moved slowly. Why that should be, he could not rightly say. He would have thought it would be the other way around.

The hiss of burning grass, the crunch of the grazing oxen, the distant yip of a coyote, these were the sounds that greeted the falling twilight. Flavius climbed down to sit near the fire, where it was warmer.

Davy took Liz and walked off, mentioning, "I'll try and rustle something up for supper."

"A bull buffalo would be nice," Flavius quipped. "And another critter for the rest of you."

The patter of feet brought Davy around. "What do you think you're doing, young lady?"

"Going with you," Becky said brightly. "My mom gave permission."

Heather was framed at the back of the wagon. Smiling, she waved.

Davy hesitated. Finding game would be difficult enough. The girl would make too much noise.

"Please, Mr. Crockett," Becky said. "I'm sick and tired of being stuck in that stuffy old wagon." She grasped his left hand. "I promise I'll behave myself. I just want to get some exercise, is all."

Against his better judgement, Davy nodded and resumed walking. She fell into step beside him, taking two strides for each one of his, her limp not overly apparent. "If you get tired, you're to tell me," Davy said.

"Pshaw. I can probably walk you into the ground. My dad used to say that I'm a bundle of energy."

"Do tell." Davy grinned. They were hunting, and by rights they should keep quiet. But here was a golden opportunity to learn more, and he could not let it pass. "So tell me. How do you feel about going to Oregon?"

"If it makes my mom happy, I'll be happy."

"What about *you*?"

Becky tore the top of a blade of grass off and stuck the end into her mouth. "I'll miss my friends. Katherine, most of all. She sat next to me at school."

"Will you miss your grandfather?"

"Grandpa Dugan?" Becky's features clouded. "No, I won't miss him one teeny bit. He was nice once but now he's mean all the time. He's trying to hurt my mom."

"Just because she likes Jon?"

Becky chewed on the grass a while. "I shouldn't say this. Mom would be upset. Grandpa Dugan didn't like my dad much, either. I heard them yelling one night. It was terrible."

Davy felt guilty about coaxing the child into revealing family secrets, but he let her go on.

"Grandpa Dugan told my mom that my dad wasn't

good enough for her. That she should have married the man Grandpa Dugan wanted her to marry.''

"How did your mother take that?"

"Oh, you should have heard her!" Becky squealed. "She used the kind of words I'm never allowed to say. She was screaming at Grandpa Dugan and he was hollering at her. I tried to sleep by pulling a pillow over my head, but it didn't help.''

"This was before your father passed on?"

"Sure was. That very next day I saw my dad and Grandpa Dugan off by themselves. My dad was real angry and he pushed Grandpa a few times. I got out of there before they saw me.''

Davy had a lot of questions, but they had to wait. A rabbit bounded across their path and was gone with a flash of bobbing tail. Davy brought Liz to bear a shade too slow. The rabbit blended into the grass on their left.

"Get him!" Becky urged.

Davy started to run in pursuit, then realized the blunder he was committing and stopped and waited for the girl to catch up. Snatching her hand, he hastened in the direction the rabbit had gone.

Becky was aglow with excitement. She mimicked his every movement, stopping when he did. She was so sweet and lively and dutiful that it reminded him of his own children, and an intense hankering to see them again came over him. He had not been so deeply homesick in weeks.

A burst of motion signaled the rabbit's flight. Davy tried to fix a bead, but the animal was moving much too rapidly. He forged on, stopping every half dozen yards to crouch and peer into the grass. Becky imitated everything he did, making no more noise than he did. She was a gem.

They covered several hundred feet without spotting the rabbit again. Davy had almost decided that it had eluded them when the grass to the right rustled. Crouching, he sighted down the barrel at an object low to the ground, twenty feet away. It moved. His finger curled on the trigger and he was a heartbeat from firing when the outline of the object resolved itself into something other than a rabbit.

It was a human foot.

Davy stiffened. Lowering the rifle, he wrapped an arm around Becky and jerked her down lower to the ground. Her cry of surprise was stifled by the hand he clamped over her mouth. Nodding at the foot, he whispered, "Be still."

To her credit, Becky did not panic. She saw it and tensed. Clamping her mouth shut, she nodded to show that she understood.

Davy could see a pair of moccasins now, cut low, just above the ankle. The legs they were attached to were spindly. He began to back up when he distinguished another pair of legs to the left. Damn his stupidity! he fumed. He had been so amused by the girl and so caught up in the chase that he had blundered into a hunting party—or worse, a war party.

The crucial question was: Which tribe? His knowledge of the prairie dwellers was slim. From the stories told back in Tennessee, the plains were crawling with hostiles hell-bent to wipe out every white who set foot in their territory—tribes like the Cheyenne, the Arapahos, and the Blackfeet. But he had no clear idea of where each tribe could be found. The prairie was one giant question mark.

"Back off slowly," Davy whispered into Becky's ear.

She molded herself to him as he retreated, her fingers digging into his leg.

The Indian on the left moved on a parallel course. Davy tried to see more of the warrior but the thick grass hindered him. He could solve the mystery of the man's identity by standing up, but that would expose him to an arrow or a lance.

Davy would not have been quite so worried had he been alone. Given his druthers, he would prefer to talk his way out of trouble rather than resort to violence. It had worked with the Chippewas and the Lakotas. But he had the child to think of. Gambling with his life was one thing; under no circumstances would he risk hers.

Suddenly the Indian on the right broke into motion, paralleling them also. Davy suspected that the pair were going to close in eventually, but the warriors kept their distance. After traveling the better part of a hundred yards, Davy drew up short. If he continued on, he would lead them right to the wagon.

Slanting to the southwest, Davy deliberately made enough noise for the two warriors to hear. He tramped another half dozen heavy-footed steps, then hunkered, pulling Becky down beside him.

The ploy worked. The two Indians continued on, and when they had gone twenty feet, Davy seized Becky's wrist and bolted into the grass at a right angle to the warriors.

Right away, yips broke out, reminiscent of hunting coyotes.

Davy did not need to look to know that the two warriors had given chase. Becky was doing her utmost to keep up with him, but her shorter legs hampered her. In order to gain ground, Davy scooped the girl into his arms and whispered, "Don't worry. I'll get you out of this scrape, princess."

Plunging into the grass, Davy ran for all he was worth. Blades of grass slashed his neck and cheeks. Stems cut his hands, his wrists. Yet he did not slow down. Loud crashing was all the proof he needed that the warriors were after him. They had thrown caution to the wind.

Davy poured on the speed, running as swiftly as possible while balancing Becky in his arms and holding onto Liz.

He had to gauge the timing of his next move carefully. Too soon or too late heightened the prospect of being discovered. With an ear to the swish of grass in his wake, Davy took another four bounds, stopped on the head of a pin, and dropped flat. Instantly, he wriggled to the right approximately eight feet. Rolling onto his side, he placed a hand on the butt of a flintlock. Now all he could do was pray.

In moments the grass crackled and shook. The warriors were flying to overtake him. He glimpsed a swarthy, skinny figure going past, but could make out few details. As soon as the footsteps faded, he was on his feet and barreling southward.

"You did it," Becky said, elated. "You're as sneaky as a fox, Mr. Crockett."

Davy was flattered. He did not see fit to mention that he had been much *too* sneaky when he was her age. Forever skipping school. Forever ducking out of chores. Always sneaking off to hunt when he should have been working. Of all the Crockett boys, he had been the naughtiest. The wonder of it was that his pa hadn't disowned him.

Neither Indian reappeared. In five minutes, Davy saw

fit to lower Becky, who smoothed her dress, then massaged the scar on her leg.

"That must have hurt something awful," Davy commented while scanning the prairie.

"Did it ever," Becky said. "I got it when my dad died."

"You were with him?"

Becky nodded. "It happened on one of Grandpa Dugan's steamboats. My dad was helping to load some crates. A big net broke and they fell on top of him." Sadness choked off her account.

"There's no need to go on."

"I don't mind," Becky responded. "There's not much more to tell, anyway." She pointed at her scar. "One of the crates tipped over and pinned me. My leg was broken. The doctor thought I'd never walk again, but I showed him."

"Your mother must be very proud of you."

"I'm more proud of her. She stood up to Grandpa Dugan when he wouldn't let us go. And she didn't marry that horrible Mr. Alcott."

"Who?"

"Horace Alcott. He's a good friend of Grandpa Dugan's. Grandpa wanted my mother to marry him, but she wouldn't give in." Becky folded her arms across her chest. "A good thing, too. Mr. Alcott wasn't very nice. He doesn't like kids, so he was always shooing me off."

"What was your father's first name?"

"Tom. Thomas Fitzgerald. But Grandpa doesn't like mom to use that name, so she goes by Dugan."

What a charmer, Davy thought. As they hurried on, he reconstructed the sequence of events, getting them straight in his head.

Heather Dugan had married Tom Fitzgerald against

her stepfather's wishes. Alexander Dugan, for some un-known reason, had despised the man, yet had given Fitz-gerald a job with one of his shipping lines. An accident later claimed Fitzgerald's life.

Next Dugan had the gall to try to coerce his step-daughter into marrying Alcott, but somewhere along the line Heather had fallen in love anew, with Jonathan Hamlin. Now the pair were fleeing to the Oregon Coun-try to escape her stepfather and start over with a clean slate.

Davy had never met Alexander Dugan, but already he despised the man. What sort of father, stepfather or no, would seek to force a grieving widow to wed someone she did not care for? What sort of human being felt he had the God-given right to impose his will on everyone else, and damn the consequences?

The plain and simple truth, as his ma used to say, was that some people were too big for their britches.

Although the prairie was quiet, Davy stayed alert. The Indians might still be in the area. He was glad he had made the fire so small. It gave off so little smoke that he was confident the warriors would not spot it.

"Look there, Mr. Crockett."

Becky's finger stabbed forward. Davy was flabber-gasted to behold a thin grey column spiraling skyward. Someone had added fuel to the fire!

"Come on!" Grasping her hand, Davy flew. He got so carried away that he nearly yanked Becky off her feet. Chafing at her slow speed, he picked her up again.

"What's your hurry, Mr. Crockett?"

"The Indians," Davy said, and let it go at that.

"We'd have heard shots or yells if the wagon was being attacked, wouldn't we?"

That was true. Davy slowed, pacing himself. He was

getting worked up over nothing. Nevertheless, he was vastly relieved when he burst into the camp.

The wagon sat undisturbed. The oxen and the horse were where they should be. Flames burned brightly in the darkening twilight, but Flavius was no longer by the fire. Figuring that his friend had climbed back inside, Davy called out softly, "We're back."

Becky squealed.

For around the front of the wagon had come six armed warriors.

Chapter Six

Davy Crockett stepped between Becky and the warriors and took aim at the foremost. Through his mind filtered images of Flavius and Heather being caught off guard, of knives sinking into their bodies, of them being dragged into the grass and hidden. He tucked Liz to his shoulder, thumbed back the hammer, and was applying his finger to the trigger when it dawned on him that the warriors were just standing there, staring. Not one made any effort to employ a weapon.

Davy held off firing. Raising his head, he studied the Indians. They were not the most impressive bunch he had ever laid eyes on. Small in stature compared to the Lakotas, they were generally thin and wiry, plainly adorned in skimpy buckskin loincloths and low moccasins. Five of the six carried short bows and had small quivers strapped to their sides. The last man, the tallest, held a fine lance decorated with feathers and beads. Davy had a hunch that the lance had either been received in trade with another tribe, or been taken from an enemy in combat.

The man with the lance advanced a few paces. Older than the others, he had a wrinkled, weathered face. Smiling, he held up his hand, palm out, and said something in low, guttural tones.

Davy lowered Liz. The Indians appeared friendly enough, but what had happened to Flavius and Heather? As if in answer to his unspoken query, his partner stuck his head out the back of the wagon.

"You're back! Thank goodness!"

Flavius Harris had been startled half out of his wits when the six warriors showed up. He had been hunkered beside the fire, warming his hurt side, when a feeling had come over him that he was being watched. Chalking it up to bad nerves, he had shifted and been dumbfounded to find the six Indians lined up just inside the circle of firelight.

Since the warrior had made no hostile moves, neither did Flavius. Holding his rifle, he had backed to the wagon and climbed in to protect Heather and Hamlin.

The Indians had filed around the wagon a few times, examining the tongue and the wheels and commenting among themselves, then moved to one side and just stood there, as if waiting.

Now Flavius hopped to the ground, ignoring the pain that flared. "I don't know what these fellers want," he told Davy. "I don't think they speak a lick of English. And I don't savvy that finger talk, like you do."

Davy cradled Liz. During his stay with the Nadowessioux, he had learned enough of the peculiar sign language that seemed to be used by most tribes to get by. Moving toward the warrior with the lance, he signed, "Sunset, day, good." There were no signs for *hello* or

od evening that he knew of, so he did the best he
uld, adding, "We friends."

The warrior's smile widened. "Friends," he signed,
d launched into a fluid flurry of hand gestures that was
fficult for Davy to follow. The gist was that the Indians
me in peace.

Davy thanked him. "Question. You people called?"

Again the warrior used sign, but it was a gesture new
Davy and he shook his head to signify as much. The
dian spoke aloud. "Kanza," he said, and tapped his
est. "Kanza."

Davy had never heard of them. He was going to in-
ire where they were from when Heather showed her-
f, a pistol in hand.

"I gather it's safe for me to come down?"

The warriors betrayed great surprise. Some started to-
rd the wagon, but stopped at a word from their leader.
Flavius was ready to shoot if any of them made a
ong move. He did not trust Indians as much as Davy
l, and he didn't see how Davy could, since Indians
d butchered Davy's grandfather, whom Davy had
ored.

Flavius figured that it had something to do with the
he Davy had been out hunting and been stricken by
 strange illness that afflicted him now and then. In-
ns had found him and taken him to a Quaker woman
o had nursed him back to health. If not for those
dians, Davy would surely have perished.

"I had her keep low," Flavius now mentioned. "They
dn't know she was in there."

Grasping Becky's hand, Davy circled to the wagon,
st to be safe. White women were a rarity on the plains,
d he was unsure how the warriors would react. Some

tribes, like the Comanche, were notorious for steal[ing]
women.

The Kanza men talked excitedly but made no threatening moves. They were fascinated by Heather's gold[en]
hair, pointing at it again and again and whispering [ex]citedly. She was probably the first blond person they h[ad]
ever encountered.

"Stay in there a while yet," Davy cautioned, planti[ng]
himself next to the loading gate.

"I need water for Jon," Heather said. "He's fev[er]ish."

"I'll fetch it, Ma," Becky volunteered.

Davy held onto her. "No. Let Flavius."

The Indians had calmed down but Flavius did not tu[rn]
his back to them as he sidled around the wagon to [the]
water barrel. After filling the dipper, he brought it [to]
Heather.

Davy reckoned that these were the same warriors [he]
had bumped into out on the prairie. Was their frien[d]ness sincere or feigned? Some Indians were not abo[ve]
pretending to be peaceful, then turning savage wh[en]
their white hosts least expected it.

The older warrior came forward. He touched the t[ips]
of the first and second fingers of his right hand to [his]
mouth, then elevated his right index finger, the back fa[c]ing out, in front of his face. It was the sign for *broth[er]*.

Davy was inclined to believe him until the warr[ior]
abruptly lowered a hand to the knife at his waist. Da[vy]
tensed. The warrior slowly drew the knife, reversed [his]
grip, and held it out to Davy, hilt first. The meaning w[as]
crystal clear.

Davy touched the hilt but did not take the weap[on.]
The warrior replaced it, content. "Question. Y[ou]
called?" Davy signed.

GET YOUR 4 FREE BOOKS NOW—
A VALUE BETWEEN $16 AND $20

Mail the Free Book Certificate Today!

FREE BOOKS CERTIFICATE!

YES! I want to subscribe to the Leisure Western Book Club. Please send my 4 FREE BOOKS. Then, each month, I'll receive the four newest Leisure Western Selections to preview FREE for 10 days. If I decide to keep them, I will pay the Special Members Only discounted price of just $3.36 each, a total of $13.44. This saves me between $3 and $6 off the bookstore price. There are no shipping, handling or other charges. There is no minimum number of books I must buy and I may cancel the program at any time. In any case, the 4 FREE BOOKS are mine to keep—at a value of between $17 and $20! Offer valid only in the USA.

Name_____

Address_____

City_____ State_____

Zip_____ Phone_____

Biggest Savings Offer!

For those of you who would like to pay us in advance by check or credit card—we've got an even bigger savings in mind. Interested? Check here. ☐

If under 18, parent or guardian must sign.
Terms, prices and conditions subject to change. Subscription subject to acceptance. Leisure Books reserves the right to reject any order or cancel any subscription.

GET FOUR BOOKS TOTALLY *FREE*—A VALUE BETWEEN $16 AND $20

PLEASE RUSH
MY FOUR FREE
BOOKS TO ME
RIGHT AWAY!

Leisure Western Book Club
P.O. Box 6613
Edison, NJ 08818-6613

demanded. "That's ours, in case it's slipped your mind."

The Kanza looked at her, then at the blanket. Her words were foreign, but her tone was not. White Feather took his hands off the blanket.

"Now you've gone and upset him," Davy said. To appease the warrior, he beamed and placed White Feather's hands back on the gift.

"So?"

"So we need him as a friend, and the surest way to prove to an Indian that you're friendly is to give him something." Davy indicated the pile of blankets and used her own statement against her. "In case it's slipped your mind, blankets are the one thing you have plenty of. You can spare one, easily."

"I suppose it can't hurt."

White Feather unfolded the blanket, draped it over his shoulder, and left the wagon. Head high, shoulders squared, he paraded in front of the other men showing off his new prize.

"They're simpletons, aren't they?" Heather said.

A naive remark, by any standard. Once, Davy had been the same as most whites, and believed that the only good Indian was a dead one. He had despised them as vermin, as two-legged animals that deserved to be exterminated. A cruel outlook, yet a popular one, shared by no less a personage than Andrew Jackson, hero of the Creek War and prominent politician. Jackson rated the red race as grossly inferior, and advocated removing the Indians from all lands east of the Mississippi, whether the Indians wanted to go or not.

Experience had taught Davy that Indians were little different than whites. There were bad ones, sure, just as there were bad whites. But many were decent and peaceful, sharing many of the hopes and aspirations of the whites who loathed them. He would never forget those who saved his life in Tennessee, nor the kind couple who had befriended him in the Lakota village.

"They're no more simple than we are," Davy said testily. "I'll bet you preen in front of a mirror when you try on a new dress. And spend half an hour every morning combing your hair."

"What's gotten into you? I didn't mean it as an insult."

Jonathan Hamlin nipped their dispute in the bud by groaning and opening his watery eyes. "Heather?" he croaked.

"Right here, dearest." She clasped his hand to her chest and mopped his face with the damp cloth. "Be still. You need to rest."

"I'm burning inside," Jonathan said.

"You have a high fever. We're doing the best we can."

"I can't think straight. Why can't I see? Why is it so dark?"

Heather glanced at Davy in alarm. "Don't you remember? My stepfather sent Benchley after us."

"Benchley?" Jonathan said, and stuck a swollen tongue between parched lips. Brow knitting, he grimaced in torment. "Why do I hurt so? Oh, I feel so sickly."

"Quiet, now," Heather said, caressing his forehead. "We'll have you fit as a fiddle in no time. But you must sleep, beloved. Sleep for as long as you like."

Soothed by her caresses and her melodious voice, Jonathan closed his eyes, gave out a long sigh, and slipped into slumber. Heather bent her head, her hair concealing her face. "God in heaven. Why did this have to happen? Now, of all times?"

Davy went to comfort her, but someone beat him to
t. Into the wagon rushed Becky, to embrace Heather and
ay over and over, "Everything will be all right, Ma.
Everything will be all right."

A daughter comforting her mother. The irony of the
oles being reversed was not lost on Davy as he left the
wagon.

Flavius had not budged. Someone had to keep an eye
on the Indians, he felt, and since Davy was too trusting
or their mutual good, the task fell to him. Since the
chief emerged, the warriors had been jabbering among
hemselves. "All's quiet," he reported.

"They won't hurt us," Davy said.

"I wish I shared your confidence." Flavius meant it.
But he had lost kin and close friends during the clash
with the Creeks, and he wasn't about to trust a red man
fully ever again.

"Hamlin's in a bad way. He might not last the night."

Flavius knew he should be upset, but for the life of
him, he wasn't. It was selfish of him, he knew, but Ham-
in's death would ensure their immediate departure for
St. Louis. "They never should have come out here. Bet-
er if they'd gone east instead of west."

"They did what they thought was best," Davy said
n their defense. Which, when all was said and done,
was all anyone could do. Life was a series of decisions,
one right after the other. Make the right one, and all was
well. Make the wrong one, and pay the price. Everyone
went through that.

"So did we when we went on this damned gallivant,"
Flavius reminded him. "And look at where it's gotten
us."

"We're still alive and kicking," Davy said trying to
make light of their perilous escapades.

Ever the pessimist, Flavius responded, "For how much longer?" He gazed longingly to the southeast. "I tell you, after we get back, I'm going to get down on my knees and thank the Almighty for our deliverance."

"Matilda will be happy. She's always wanted you to be more religious."

"Poke fun all you want. The truth is, most husbands get to heaven by way of their wives' apron strings."

The grass nearby rustled. Davy and Flavius both spun. Out of the night jogged the two Kanzas, one bearing two plants that had been torn out of the earth by their roots. These were given to White Feather, who in turn brought them to the Tennesseans.

"Man have wound," the leader signed. "Make—" and here he used a variety of signs that, in their proper sequence, were the symbols for *plant, leaf, drink,* and *good.*

Davy gathered that the chief was advising them to concoct a tea from the leaves. He thanked White Feather and set about filling a pot with water and setting it on a tripod over the fire. A young warrior who looked barely old enough to be out of his teens hovered over Davy like a shadow, adding grass to the flames and taking the dipper from his hand to fill the pot.

The Kanzas were astonished by the water barrel. Once they learned what it was, every few minutes one of them would get up and treat himself to a drink. It got to the point where Davy had to sign to White Feather that no more should be taken without his approval.

Toward midnight, the warriors turned in. They simply rolled up on the ground and fell asleep. Davy expected White Feather to cover himself with the blanket, but the leader neatly folded it and fashioned a small bed of grass for it to lie on.

Flavius covered his mouth and snickered. "Look at him. He must not want to get it dirty. Doesn't he know it can keep him warm?"

From the scant information Davy had gleaned, he reckoned that the Kanzas were a poor tribe, not rich in horses and hides like the Sioux and others. That blanket might well be White Feather's most prized possession, comparable to a white man's poke of gold, or a favorite weapon. He said as much.

"You scare me sometimes, pard," Flavius stated.

"In what way?"

"You have this silly habit of always putting yourself into other people's heads."

"To understand someone, you have to walk in their moccasins a spell."

Flavius fluttered his lips. "That's just it, pard. Sometimes people do things for reasons other than we think." He lowered his voice. "Take Alexander Dugan, for instance. Hamlin and Heather claim that he's in the wrong. But who's to say that they're not? We have no idea why Dugan's really after them."

"Are you saying they don't deserve our help?"

"No. Not with the man blind as a bat. I'm just saying that you shouldn't become too attached to them. Sooner or later we'll be parting ways." Secretly, Flavius was afraid that his friend's fondness for being a Good Samaritan would result in a lot more hardship. Hardship he could do without.

Davy stepped to the back of the wagon. Heather had draped a blanket over the opening for privacy. Muted whispers told him they were still awake. "How is Jonathan?" he asked softly.

The blanket parted. "He's sleeping soundly enough,"

Heather reported. "His fever is still awful high, though."

"It's too soon for the medicine to take effect yet. By morning, we should see a change."

Heather placed her hand on his. "I wish there were some way of properly expressing my gratitude for all you've done. Without you we'd be helpless."

Davy wondered if she had overheard Flavius. "Don't worry. We're not about to desert you in your hour of need."

A few yards away, Flavius frowned and muttered under his breath, "Damnation. He's doing it again."

"Where will you sleep?" Heather asked.

Flavius opened his mouth to say that he would prefer to sleep inside, but he was not quick enough.

"We wouldn't want to inconvenience you," Davy said. "Under the wagon will do right fine." As an afterthought, he added, "If you can spare a few blankets, we'd be obliged."

The wind had picked up, as it usually did at night on the open prairie. Flavius knelt and eased under the wagon, careful not to put too such weight on his hurt side. Davy spread out the blankets, two for each of them.

Crawling under his, Flavius slid both pistols from under his belt and set one on either side. His rifle went next to the flintlock on his right, his knife beside the pistol on his left. All he had to do was move either hand a few inches and a weapon was in ready reach.

"I tell you," Flavius whispered, "sleeping with those Kanza out there makes my skin crawl. What's to stop them from slitting our throats in the middle of the night?"

"Nothing," Davy admitted.

"Just what I wanted to hear."

Davy removed his coonskin cap, adjusted his blanket, and propped his head on his hands. Until that moment he had not appreciated how bone-weary he was. The events of the day had drained him.

He had to be careful. Those strange bouts of illness to which he was susceptible always struck when he was run down. That first time, back in Tennessee, he had traveled fifty miles in twelve hours, chasing lost horses. The toll had nearly killed him.

Fatigue lulled him into dreamland within minutes. He slept soundly, the sleep of the weary, awakening shortly before sunrise. Crawling out into the open, he rose stiffly and stretched. Shades of pink and orange banded the eastern horizon, a prelude to dawn.

Davy stretched, then turned to collect fuel for a fire. He was nonplussed to see that the Kanzas already had a small fire going. Or, rather, three of them did, for the other three were missing.

White Feather sat wrapped in his new blanket. Grinning, he beckoned, then signed, "Sunrise, day, good." To accent his point, he inhaled deeply.

"Yes," Davy signed by holding his right hand at shoulder height with the index finger extended and his thumb on the second finger, then swinging the hand down and to the left while simultaneously pressing his index finger against his thumb.

Suddenly the three missing warriors reappeared, hurrying from the grass to confer with their leader. White Feather rose. "You come us village," he signed brusquely.

Davy was taken aback. Go to their village? "Why?" he signed.

White Feather said words in his own tongue to the

warriors, then answered, "No time talk. Arise woman. Arise fat man. Go now."

Forgetting himself, Davy said in English, "Not so fast. What's this all about?"

White Feather clapped his hands. In a blur, four of the Kanzas smoothly notched arrows to their sinew strings and swung the barbed tips toward Davy.

"Now," White Feather insisted.

Chapter Seven

The oxen plodded to the northwest as they had for the past three days. Tireless mountains of muscle that they were, they were unaffected by the blazing sun and swarms of insects. They could plod on forever, provided enough forage and water were available.

The former was easy to supply. The high grass, so abundant in the vicinity of the Mississippi, had given way to shorter sweet grass, on which the oxen thrived. Rich green, brightened by patches of enchanting wind-flowers, the prairie was more beautiful than the paint-brush of man could ever capture on canvas.

Not that Davy Crockett noticed it all that much. He had other matters on his mind—more important matters. Such as how to escape from the Kanzas, who had turned out to be as treacherous as the Comanches.

White Feather's band had disarmed Davy and Flavius, confiscated all the weapons from the wagon, and bundled them into a blanket. It was so heavy that two warriors were required to carry it. They took turns, White Feather as well.

Oddly, the Indians had not appropriated the guns or knives for their own. Nor had any of them claimed the bay. Which mystified Davy. As did their behavior in general. The Kanzas were the friendliest captors anyone had ever been taken captive by. Not once had they abused him or any of the others. Not once had they spoken angrily or hit anyone or bothered to tie Flavius and him up, even at night. He did not know what to make of it.

Davy tried to learn where they were going. But to all the sign entreaties he made, White Feather would only respond, "Explain time-in-front." Which meant that the chief would tell him at some point in the future.

One of the Kanzas was always gone, day and night. They rotated in this, too; when each man came back, the next immediately took off, running at full speed. No explanation was offered.

Heather rarely left the wagon. She was furious at the betrayal, and railed whenever White Feather entered to check on Jonathan, as he did several times daily. The Kanzas kept her supplied with medicinal tea, brewing a new batch each night.

Becky was not as flustered by the development. Davy liked to think it was because she did not realize the gravity of the situation. But then, small children naturally took calamity more in stride than adults.

Flavius was in another sulk. Most of the time he rode on the 'lazy seat,' a board attached to the side of the wagon. As glum as a rainy day, he glared at the Kanzas a lot and muttered lusty oaths.

Now it was the morning of the fourth day. They had been underway for a couple of hours when Flavius griped, "How much longer are these heathens going to keep this up?"

His shoulder was feeling better but his mood was as sour as a lemon, and Flavius could not help it. Every yard took them further from their canoe—further from home. He was so frustrated, he wanted to scream. Or beat the Kanzas senseless.

Davy walked beside the rear oxen, holding the whip. To a degree, he shared his friend's disappointment. But they were still alive, and so long as breath remained, there was hope. "White Feather won't tell me," he said. "They're taking us to their village, so it depends on how far it is."

"I'll never trust a redskin for the rest of my born days," Flavius said. "Not one of them is reliable. Every last one would as soon stab a white man in the back as look at him."

"Don't be so quick to judge."

"Quick?" Flavius snorted. "We gave them the benefit of the doubt, and look at where it got us! We should have ordered them to light a shuck for somewhere else that first night they showed up. Or shot them dead."

"In cold blood?"

"Indians massacre whites all the time for no other reason than they're white."

"And whites slaughter Indians for the same reason. But that doesn't make either side right."

Flavius exaggerated a sigh. "And the Good Lord knows that a member of the Crockett clan would never want to do anything that is *wrong*, now would he?"

"Has anyone ever told you that you're grumpy in the morning?"

"Grumpy, hell. I'm mad enough to spit nails. Being

taken captive does that to me. Call it a silly trait of the Harris clan.''

Flavius saw that his sarcasm had hurt his friend, and regretted being so callous. But Davy had brought this down on them by being too trusting—once again. Flavius despaired of Crockett ever learning that some folks just couldn't be trusted—never, ever. Blood would tell, as the old saw had it. Not all the wishful thinking in the world could change a killer into a saint.

Davy spied a flock of sparrows winging westward. They perked his interest. Sparrows were partial to trees, and trees generally grew along brooks and rivers. They were low on water, very low. Unless they found some in the next day or so, the oxen would begin to falter.

Small fingers brushed his hand. Davy looked down into Becky's grinning features. In her hand was a blue flower which she held up.

''For you. I just picked it.''

''Thank you, princess.'' Davy angled the long slender stem through the hair above his ear, then pressed his coonskin cap down to hold it in place. ''How do I look?''

''Dandy,'' Becky said, giggling. ''You're the prettiest man around.''

''A word of advice, little one. Men aren't *pretty*. They're *handsome*.''

''What's the difference? They both mean good-looking.''

Davy was hardly an expert on definitions. His limited schooling barely enabled him to read and write—if you could call the scrawls he put on paper writing. His letters always contrived to resemble the scratchings made in dirt by chickens inebriated on corn mash. ''It's a convention, is all,'' he lamely explained.

"What's that?"

"Conventions are the normal way folks do things. For instance, men wear pants and women don't. Some men grow beards and women don't. They're conventions."

"I've seen women wear pants."

"Well, so have I. But not many."

"So conventions can be changed, can't they?"

"I reckon. They're not ironclad."

"Then if I want to call a man *pretty*, I can."

Davy chuckled. "Too bad there aren't any women in politics. When you grow up, you'd make a right fine congressman or senator."

"Why aren't there any women?"

How should he answer? Davy asked himself. With the truth, or sugarcoat it? "Think of life as one big wagon. Men have hogged the reins for so long, they don't want to give them up."

"That's not fair."

"No one ever claimed life would be, princess. It's a growing process. Just like trees and the grass grow, so do we. But where they send their roots deeper, we get smarter. Or we should, if our thinkers haven't turned to fat from never being used."

Becky laughed. "You talk funny at times, Mr. Crockett. You know that?"

The Irishman and the girl made small talk until noon. Mainly she talked and he listened. He learned that her father had worked at a number of jobs before going to work for Alexander Dugan, and that it had bothered Becky, because the family never lived in any one place for very long. She would no sooner make a friend or two than the family would up and move again.

The impression he had was of a deeply unhappy childhood. "I'm sorry it was that way," he commented.

Becky shrugged. "So was I, for the longest while. But now my mom and Jon are together, and we're going to go to the Oregon Country and live in a wonderful house forever and ever. I'll have all the friends I could ever want." Clasping her hands, she cast glowing eyes to the heavens. "I'll be so glad."

The sun was directly overhead when one of the Kanza warriors pointed straight ahead and said something that excited the others.

Davy looked, but saw nothing out of the ordinary. However, in another few minutes, a ragged line of objects appeared on the horizon, objects that grew in size and clarity to become a belt of trees.

Flavius slid off the lazy seat. "Must be water," he declared. Like Davy, he had been concerned about their dwindling supply.

White Feather sent the youngest warrior on at a brisk trot. That left four, and two of them were carrying the bundled weapons.

Davy dragged his heels, drifting toward his companion. "This is our chance," he whispered. "If we can get our hands on our guns . . ."

The thought did not need to be finished. Flavius glanced at the pair with the bundle, then at White Feather and the fourth warrior, who were on the other side of the oxen. "How do you want to play it?"

"We could use a distraction," Davy said, and was as surprised as Flavius when Becky blossomed at their side. "I can help."

Flavius motioned her away. "No. It's too dangerous. Go inside with your ma."

"You're both spoilsports," Becky said. Sticking her tongue at Flavius, she skipped toward the front of the team, her limp barely noticeable. Humming merrily, she went past the lead oxen.

White Feather called out. The Kanza had made it plain that no one was to stray far from the wagon. When Becky did not heed him, the chief hurried to catch her. The other warrior trailed along.

The pair carrying the bundle slowed to watch. They were smiling, amused at the child's antics, and neither seemed to care that Davy and Flavius had strayed behind the wagon and were close to them.

Davy saw Becky zigzagging to elude White Feather, who was grinning. The Indians were being playful, not threatening. Bending, he whispered urgently, "*Now!*"

Flavius pounced on the nearest Kanza. In order not to open his wound, he lashed out with a leg rather than a fist, catching the warrior across the shins. Yelping, the man crashed down.

The second warrior had the reflexes of a panther. Releasing his burden, he skipped aside, dodging a fist Davy threw at his jaw. Davy closed in, anticipating stiff resistance, but the Kanza danced backward, holding both hands out and saying the same word over and over.

In another moment, Davy had the bundle undone and was holding one of his pistols. Cocking the hammer, he pointed it at the Kanza on the ground, who yipped and scuttled off.

The yell brought White Feather and the last warrior. They hastened back, neither attempting to unlimber their bows or draw a knife. Halting ten feet away, White Feather signed, "No quarrel! No quarrel!"

Flavius claimed his rifle. Checking it, he turned it on the leader. "I should blow a hole in him, the ornery polecat."

Davy grabbed the barrel. "No. They didn't harm us. We'll let them go if they back down."

White Feather came forward, gesturing frantically. "Peace! No fight! Indian friend."

"What's he flapping his fingers about?" Flavius asked.

"He doesn't want any trouble."

"Then tell him and the rest to skedaddle."

The two warriors who had been responsible for the bundle had joined their fellows. A heated exchange erupted, White Feather against the other three. At last the leader prevailed, but the others were none too pleased. White Feather faced around. "Gun grass. We no injure."

Davy signed an emphatic, "No!" He was not going to put the weapons down. "Go," he added. "No friend. You no true." He had accused the leader of not speaking with a straight tongue, of being deceitful. "You bad heart."

A lanky warrior gripped White Feather's arm and motioned for them to leave but White Feather was stubborn. Taking another step, he signed, "Give me gun. Go with us."

Davy signed that he would not. White Feather came closer. Violence was on the verge of breaking out when a shrill cry intruded.

"Mr. Crockett! Help me! I'm stuck!"

All this while, the wagon had continued westward, the oxen lumbering dumbly onward, since no one had commanded them to halt. In their path was Becky, desperately tugging at her left leg.

"She's caught in a prairie dog hole," Flavius said.

Until that moment, Davy had overlooked the telltale earthen mounds that dotted the area. Praire dog villages were a common sight, best avoided, since the oxen or the bay might step into a burrow and break a leg. "Pull harder!" he yelled.

Heather appeared at the back of the wagon. "What is all the shouting about?" she hollered. "What's going on?"

Becky had gripped her ankle and was yanking with all her might. The oxen were less than ten feet from her, narrowing the gap with each ponderous stride. "Ma! Ma! Help!"

Davy couldn't believe the oxen would trample her. They were dumb brutes, but surely not *that* dumb. He bolted to her rescue as Heather swung over the gate and dropped.

"Where's my daughter? What's wrong?"

Davy flew past, not wasting a second. The team was eight feet from the girl. Then seven. He passed the rear animals and bellowed for them to stop. The oxen obeyed, but they were too massive and slow-witted to halt very quickly. The lead pair were six feet from Becky. Five. Four.

In a long leap, Davy slanted beyond them, seized Becky under the arms, and literally tore her from the prairie dog hole. She cried out as they tumbled and rolled, Davy cushioning her with his body. As they rose, he discovered that the team was standing on the exact spot she had occupied.

"Thank you," the girl said softly. "I wasn't looking where I was going."

Heather was beside herself. Sweeping the child into her arms, she blurted, "Are you all right? What was that all about? You scared me half to death."

The wagon blocked Davy's view of Flavius and the Kanzas. Hurrying around to the other side of the team, he saw Flavius on the ground, the four warriors on top. They were endeavoring to pin his arms and legs, but he was putting up stiff resistance in spite of his wound.

Davy sprinted toward them. Venting a Creek war whoop when he was close, he hurtled into the fray. Two of the warriors rose to meet him, but he bowled them over as if they were scarecrows. Spinning, he planted a solid fist on the chin of a warrior who had hold of Flavius's right arm. He was cocking his fist for another swing when the first pair piled onto him. In a whirlwind of hands and feet, they went down.

Grunting and heaving, Davy dislodged one. The other clung to him like glue. When he tried to rise, the man wrapped sinewy arms around his legs, hampering him. He punched the warrior's back, to no effect.

Somewhere, someone screamed. Davy thought it was Becky, and struggled again to regain his feet. Another Kanza smashed onto him. Driven onto his stomach, Davy felt knees gouge into his spine, into his legs. His arms were clamped in twin vises and he was roughly hoisted erect.

Nearby, Flavius was already upright, similarly held by the warrior who had been with White Feather and another warrior whom Davy did not recognize. The significance of that eluded him until he looked up and saw that a ring of Kanzas surrounded them, some with arrows nocked to curved bows, others with drawn knives or war clubs.

White Feather was brushing off his new red blanket. Ruffled but dignified, he aligned it over his shoulder, then raised an arm aloft.

''What the hell!'' Flavius fumed. ''Where did these new ones come from?'' He was peeved at himself for being taken by surprise when he had them covered, and even more so for allowing Davy to persuade him not to shoot every one when the chance presented itself.

There were seventeen, all told, various ages, attired in virtually identical loincloths and moccasins. At White Feather's insistence, their weapons were lowered. Davy and Flavius were released, the guns were gathered up, and in due course they were on the move again, now guarded by six warriors apiece.

Heather and Becky had been escorted to the wagon. Becky was peering out the front. "I tried to warn you," she said. "They came out of nowhere."

That was not quite the case, as Davy and Flavius were to learn when they reached the trees. Verdant vegetation lined a shallow river, and along its bank had been erected over forty small lodges, crafted from slim willow poles layered with hides, straw, and dirt.

"Hovels," Flavius branded them.

Davy had to admit that the huts were a poor excuse for human habitation. Flimsy and filthy, they were utterly unlike the regal, picturesque buffalo-hide lodges of the Lakotas and the sturdy wigwams of the Chippewas. His hunch that the Kanzas were a poor tribe had not done them justice; they were *miserably* poor.

They were also crop growers. Plots of beans, pumpkins, corn, and other vegetables had been sown. Narrow irrigation ditches diverted water. Poor though they were, the Kanzas were clever and resourceful.

Men, women, and children gathered in the center of the village. The women were stouter than the men and scantily clad, when they were clad at all. The way the children frolicked and gambled about reminded Davy of painter cubs. They would not stop running up to him and plucking at his leggings, as if to assure themselves that he was real.

The wagon proved a marvel to the Kanzas. The entire tribe circled it, running their hands over team and bed alike.

When Heather threw back the blanket she had draped over the back and climbed down with Becky, the Kanzas were awestruck. Her blond hair shimmered in the sunlight like burnished copper, and the Kanza women could not stop feeling it and rubbing the ends between their fingers.

White Feather stood in front of a lodge slightly larger than the rest, the red blanket adorning his chest in a grand splash of color. Two older women fawned over him as he preened with head held high.

The bundle of weapons had been deposited near White Feather's hut. Davy considered trying to reach his pistols, but the hopeless odds dissuaded him. His best estimate was that the village contained three dozen warriors, another dozen older men, perhaps seventy women, and a score of children.

Flavius simmered with resentment. It wasn't bad enough being taken captive. Now he must endure the humiliation of torture and lingering death.

Visions of horrid torments filled Flavius's head, of having his ears and nose hacked off, his tongue ripped out. Of having his fingers chopped off, or his gut sliced open and his intestines used to strangle him. It had happened to others. Such gory tales were common fare at taverns in the East, tales of the barbaric heathens who occupied the uncharted West and preyed on unwary trappers, traders, and travelers.

Flavius had never figured it would happen to him. He'd looked forward to dying in his rocking chair or his bed. Peacefully, preferably painlessly.

A trio of young boys were shyly studying him. One

stuck out his stomach and waddled like a dog, eliciting gay mirth. Flavius snarled at them, but they only laughed harder.

At that point a warrior dashed into the village from the east. Most of the Kanzas were too preoccupied to notice. Davy saw the warrior run to White Feather, point at the prairie, and ramble on at length. White Feather acted pleased by the report. Clapping the warrior's shoulder, the chief came to an open space near the wagon and got everyone's attention by yipping loud and long.

The tribe listened attentively. At the conclusion of White Feather's address, the leathery Kanza walked over to the frontiersmen. "Be glad. I think hard. Trouble over."

Davy did not understand, and signed as much. The Kanza responded at length, shocking Davy.

"What is it?" Flavius coaxed.

"We're not their prisoners."

"You could have fooled me."

"We're honored guests."

"Tell this geezer his people have a mighty peculiar way of being friendly."

"That's just it. They did all this for our benefit." Davy elaborated. "A small party of Pawnees found our camp and were spying on us. The Kanzas were afraid that the Pawnees would ambush us if we went on by ourselves, so White Feather brought us here for our own protection."

Flavius was inclined to rate the story as sheer cock-and-bull if not for the sincere expression of relief worn by White Feather.

"They were watching the Pawnees this whole time.

101

The man who just arrived reported that they've gone north. The danger is over.''

''Well, now,'' Flavius said, and coughed. ''See? You shouldn't have made such a fuss when they took our guns. I knew all along that everything would turn out just fine.''

Chapter Eight

Davy Crockett liked the Kanzas. They were a simple people. Not simpleminded, as some whites would have it. Simply—simple. They delighted in the small pleasures life offered: eating, conversation, fellowship. Laughter bubbled from them as naturally as foam in rapids. A ready smile was on everyone's lips, young and old alike.

By the second day, Davy felt right at home. The Kanzas went out of their way to make him feel welcome. For example, all he had to do was express hunger and he was offered more food than he could eat. Not lavish fare, by any standard. Deer meat and rabbit were common. Vegetables were abundant.

In the evenings, the whole tribe would gather around. White Feather would ask questions of their guests, and the answers sparked mirth as often as awe. When Davy mentioned that white men floated on rivers in enormous lodges that belched smoke and steam, the village pealed

103

with gaiety. They believed he was telling a whopper of a tale, and he couldn't blame them. Some things had to be seen to be believed.

Flavius Harris did what Flavius always did best; he sulked. He was eager to return to their canoe and resume their journey down the Mississippi. Begrudgingly, he grew fond of the Kanzas, especially the children. Many of the little ones became attached to him and would follow him wherever he went. The boy who had poked fun at his belly became a second shadow, imitating everything Flavius did, from how he ate to how he scratched himself.

It helped that Flavius was allowed to eat as often and as much as he wanted. The second day there, four warriors showed up with a large buck and a doe, hung from poles. As fast as you please, women had the deer skinned and butchered and roasting over several fires at once.

Flavius was personally handed a portion of juicy haunch. He dug into it with relish, ripping off great chunks with his teeth and chewing slowly to savor the taste. His second shadow mimicked every bite, every expression. Flavius laughed and clapped the boy on the back so hard that he nearly pitched onto his face.

It was shortly after the meal, after the sun had gone down, that Davy strolled to the wagon. He rapped on the bed. The blanket was pulled aside by Becky.

"Mr. Crockett!"

"It's Davy, remember? Just plain Davy." Crockett peered past her at a lantern suspended from the frame that supported the cloth cover. "How's Jonathan faring?"

Heather came from the front, saying, "Better. Much better. His fever has broken, but he's still weak as can be." She bit her lower lip. "He still can't see, though.

I keep a compress on his head, like the old squaw told me to, but it hasn't helped any.''

The old squaw was a kind elderly woman versed in herbal remedies and other treatments. Most tribes, Davy had found, knew how to make medicine from a variety of plants. So extensive was their knowledge of what each and every plant could do, it bordered on the remarkable.

And in every tribe there was one or two who were more adept than most. Among the Lakotas, it had been a wizened man. Here among the Kanza, it happened to be a woman called Red Flower. She was spry for her age, always smiling and carefree, not minding one whit that three of her front teeth were missing. She had been kicked by a buffalo cow, Davy learned, back when she was young.

"Give it time," he told Heather. "We can stay as long as it takes."

"I don't know. Wouldn't it be better to head for St. Louis? The doctors there might be able to do a lot more for him."

Davy was blunt. "I doubt it. Even if they could, Jon is in no shape to travel. He'll need a week or more just to get his strength back."

"Another week," Heather said forlornly. Davy turned to go, but she leaned down and grasped his shirt. "I can't thank you enough for all you've done. If you hadn't come along when you did, I shudder to think what would have happened."

"We were happy to be of help," Davy said, and walked off. He had not gone six feet when Flavius seemed to pop up out of the ground.

"Did I just hear correctly? One more *week*?"

"Afraid so."

David Thompson

"At the rate we're going, I'll have white hair before I set foot in my cabin again."

"They say white hair makes a man look distinguished."

"Who says it? Those with white hair?" Flavius puffed out his cheeks and exhaled noisily. "Maybe I should learn the Kanza tongue and build me a lodge." He adopted a wry grin. "Some of the younger women ain't half bad. I could always marry one and settle down to a life of deer meat and dirt."

Davy headed for a fire, his friend falling into step. "Goodness gracious. You'd be a bigamist. One wife per customer is the general rule, as I recollect."

"I used to wonder about that," Flavius said. "I always figured the women came up with that brainstorm so there would be enough men to go around." He paused. "Now I think the men made the rule out of self-preservation."

"How's that?"

"Being hitched to one woman is enough to drive a man to drink. Being wed to two or more would drive a fellow plumb mad."

White Feather, half a dozen prominent warriors, and twice as many women and children were in a circle, listening to an ancient man relate a story. Davy had picked up a smattering of their tongue, a few words here, a few there, but not enough to get the gist of the old man's tale. He sank cross-legged beside White Feather, who wore the red blanket over both shoulders as if it were an oversize shawl.

The old man talked on. White Feather translated using sign talk. The tale had to do with the old days, back before the coming of the whites, back when the Kanza lived far to the southeast in a country where the weather

106

was always warm and they could grow crops every month of the year.

The tribe had always been small, always weaker than their neighbors. In those days, they had been under the protection of a mighty tribe that built great mounds and wore masks that shone like the sun.

These mound builders had been giants, claimed the ancient Kanza, twice the size of normal men and five times as strong. Mighty fighters, time and again they staved off incursions by other tribes into their territory.

For generation upon generation, the Kanzas had tilled the soil, giving part of each harvest to the giants who protected them. The Kanzas prospered, and were content.

Then one day the giants began to die off. The invincible warriors who could not be defeated in combat were slain by a mysterious sickness that killed them with chilling suddenness. It was rumored that the sickness had been spread by a captive, a strange paleskin who wore garments no one had ever seen and spoke in a tongue no one understood.

With the mound builders gone, the Kanzas were on their own. Hostile tribes raided them with impunity. Their situation became dire, so much so that their leaders decided to leave their homeland and seek somewhere safe to live.

The trek had been long and hard. Many perished along the way, from want of food and drink, or from the arrows and lances of roving war parties.

Decimated, the Kanzas arrived at the river that now bore their name. The region appealed to them. Game was abundant, the soil rich. They broke into bands and claimed the territory as their own. For a while, all had gone well.

The Kanzas always preferred to live in peace with their neighbors. Unfortunately, it turned out that some of their neighbors did not have the word *peace* in their vocabulary.

To the south dwelled the warlike Comanches, master horsemen, undisputed lords of their domain.

To the northwest were the Pawnees, who, like the Kanzas, cultivated the soil. But the Pawnees were warriors first and foremost. They plagued the Kanzas, raiding at will. Horses gave them an advantage the Kanzas could never overcome.

Davy asked White Feather why the Kanzas did not have horses of their own. Two reasons, the chief said. For one thing, the only way the Kanzas could obtain them would be to raid the Pawnees or the Comanches—which was certain suicide. For another, the Kanzas were intimidated by horses.

The first time the tribe had seen a man on horseback, they had thought it was some bizarre new creature, some strange fusion of human and monster.

Once, many moons ago, a band of Kanzas had found two horses wandering on the plain. They had tried to tame the pair, but the horses proved too wild. One man broke a leg, another an arm. To add insult to injury, the horses were later stolen by the Comanches.

So now the Kanzas did without. They wanted nothing to do with Hamlin's bay. Where the Lakota or Cheyenne would have taken the horse right off, the Kanzas gave it a wide berth. Davy had to see that it was fed and watered himself.

The ancient Kanza came to the end of his recital. The thrust of his story had been that while times were hard for his people, they had been a lot harder long ago. The Kanzas should be thankful, he said, for a river that never dried up, for game that never died off, and for the coming of the whites, whose trade goods were keenly sought.

White Feather turned to Davy, hands flying. The Kanzas would always welcome their white brothers with wide arms, the chief said. And they hoped that their white brothers would be equally open.

Everyone looked expectantly at Davy. Nervous under their scrutiny, he started to assure them that whites were always ready to deal honestly and peaceably with Indians. But it was a lie, of course. Any number of whites would as soon slit an Indian's throat as look at him. So Davy compromised. He told them that *he* was glad to be their friend, and that whenever he was in the area, he would stop by to trade.

As a rule, the Kanzas turned in early. By eight o'clock, most had retired to their lodges.

Davy rose and stretched his leg muscles by taking a stroll around the village perimeter. He came to the river and stood on the bank. Reflected on the surface was the full moon, the image distorted by the current. Craning his neck, he gazed skyward.

So many stars! Davy thought. City-dwellers had no idea what they were missing. Out here on the plains, the heavens swarmed with a myriad of twinkling pinpoints, too many to count, so many that it made a body's head swim to contemplate the enormity of Creation.

Davy had heard tell that with a telescope, ten times as many stars were visible. He had never looked through one, himself, but he believed it. Ten times! And there were those who believed that if a powerful enough telescope could be made, the stars would been seen to go on forever and ever.

It dazzled the senses. It made a man feel as if he were a mere speck in the giant scheme of things. As if he were a dot of dirt in the middle of the prairie, or a drop of water in the river flowing by.

A twig crunched behind him.

Automatically, Davy whirled, leveling Liz. He must have scared Becky out of two months' growth. "What are you doing out so late, young lady?"

"I couldn't sleep. I saw you walking around and decided to join you."

"Does your mother know you're here?"

"She's asleep. Passed out on Jon's chest, she was so tired." The girl stepped to the water's edge, squatted, and dipped a finger. "Cold, isn't it? Mom says I need to take a bath tomorrow. I'm liable to catch my death."

"I could use one myself," Davy said. In contrast to Flavius and most of his other backwoods friends, he was partial to bathing. He liked to feel clean. Just as he liked to be clean shaven. His friends could jest about his quirks all they wanted, but at least when he was upwind of someone, that someone wouldn't gag.

Becky swirled the water. Out of the blue, she asked, "Why do bad things happen to good people?"

"You mean Jon?"

She nodded. "He's a nice man, Mr. Crockett. He always treats me decent, and treats my mom like she's a queen." Becky rose. "Why did he have to be shot? Why did he have to go blind?"

"It's just life, princess."

"Shucks. That's no answer."

Davy propped Liz against his side and held out both fists. "Pick one."

"What for?"

"Humor me. Pick one."

The girl selected his right. "What does that prove?"

"Why did you pick that one?"

110

"I don't know. No special reason, I guess."

"The same with life. Things happen sometimes for no special reason. We might trip and bust a finger. Or we're sharpening a knife and we cut ourselves. Or maybe our horse goes wild and throws us. Any number of things can happen to us each and every day. Some of those things are good, some not so good. Like Jon being hit by the stray slug. No one planned it. It just happened."

"Like my father dying?"

"Same, same."

"You think a lot, don't you?"

"I try. My grandpa liked to say that if we used our brains half as much as we do our backsides, we'd all be as smart as Solomon." Davy held her hand. "Enough questions, little one. Let's get you to the wagon. Your ma will throw a fit if she wakes and finds you gone."

"Awwww."

All but one fire had died out. Two old warriors were the only Kanzas up. The village was tranquil, quiet. Davy led Becky to the tongue and boosted her up. "Sleep tight." To his surprise, she pecked his cheek. Then she was gone.

Warm and mushy inside, Davy sauntered to the river and resumed his stroll. In the distance, coyotes yipped. A wolf howled and was answered by another. To the northwest, a painter screeched, sounding for all the world like a woman in labor. An owl voiced the eternal query of its kind.

Davy was northeast of the village when a tiny speck of light caught his eye. It was due east, so small that he could not be confident it wasn't a star, low down on the horizon. Yet it could also be a campfire. He strained his eyes, but could not make up his mind.

Shrugging, Davy walked to the wagon. From under it

fluttered loud snoring, reminiscent of a saw chewing into cedar. Davy lay on his side, covered himself, and plugged his ear with a finger. It did no good. Flavius made more noise than a riled grizzly. Davy lightly pushed him, but all that did was cause Flavius to sputter and snort. Finally Davy shoved him, hard.

Flavius opened his eyes. Blinking sluggishly, he looked around. "What happened? Was that you?"

"You're dreaming. Go back to sleep."

"Thanks. Think I will."

In a moment, Flavius was sound asleep. But he had stopped snoring. Chuckling, Davy stretched out, making himself comfortable.

A gust of wind brought with it the sounds of night life, the yips and howls and bird cries Davy had heard a while ago.

Like the emerald hills of Tennessee, the prairie abounded with wildlife. During the day, the grass-eaters held sway, foraging to their heart's content. Predators ruled the night. Big cats and bears and wolves and more. Some were as deadly to man as they were to the four-legged quarry they hunted.

Davy drifted into sleep. Disturbing dreams troubled him. In the first, he arrived back at his cabin only to find it burned to the ground and charred skeletons scattered about. It woke him in the middle of the night. A cold sweat chilled him as he rolled onto his other side and pulled the blanket up against his chin.

The next dream was no better. He was on a sunny prairie, running for his life, being chased by a shadowy form that growled and rumbled and drummed the earth with heavy paws. Just as the thing was about to catch him, he awoke again, perspiring heavily.

ently into the woods. Davy pivoted and saw sparrows
frolicking in the brush.

White Feather emerged, the red blanket over his head
and shoulders. Only his nose, mouth, and eyes were visible. He smiled and gave a little wave, then headed for
the river.

Golden beams lit the eastern sky. In the misty haze
of early morning, the sun seemed larger somehow. A
blazing orb, a fiery furnace, a harbinger of the hot day
to come.

Becky finished filling the pot. Davy took it from her
and walked to the rear. She reached up, then stopped
and giggled when Flavius stuck his head out from under
the bed and grunted like a discontented bear.

"You should see yourself, Mr. Harris. Your hair is
sticking up every which way. What little hair you have,
anyway."

Flavius frowned at the world. "What a way to begin
a new day," he lamented.

A low growl reached Davy's ears. The mongrel was
staring into the trees again, the hackles of its neck bristling, its lips curled back. He looked and spied the sparrows, taking wing. Something had spooked them,
evidently. "What is it, boy?" he asked softly.

The answer came in the form of a thunderclap. Not a
thunderclap spawned by nature, but the collective blast
of rifles being fired simultaneously. A lot of rifles, to
judge by the din.

The village was under attack.

Chapter Nine

The first volley was devastating. Davy ducked and yanked Becky down beside him as slugs ripped into the wagon and sent sharp slivers flying.

Around them bedlam swirled. Warriors, women, even children were hit.

A tall Kanza who had raised his arms to the sky in token greeting of the new day was smashed backward by a bullet that tore into his forehead and burst out the back of his skull.

A woman carrying a jug toward the river cried out as she was struck between the shoulder blades. Arms flung outward, she smashed onto her face.

Several women returning from the river were laughing and joking one second, sprawled lifeless on the ground the next.

Two small boys, playing among the lodges, were ripped asunder by multiple shots and slumped earthward in miserable crumpled heaps.

"What the hell!" Flavius bellowed. Clutching one of
s pistols, he pointed it at the cloud of smoke that had
llowed from the undergrowth, and fired. Whether he
ought down one of the unseen raiders, he couldn't say.

For a few moments, the firing died down. The Kanza
y everywhere, women wailing, stricken children cry-
g, bloody warriors groaning.

Davy shoved Becky under the wagon beside Flavius.
s he did, the blanket above them was thrown aside.
eather filled the opening, worry for her daughter ren-
ring her careless.

"What is it? Who's doing all the shooting?"

Davy hurled himself upward. He cleared the top of
e gate and swung an arm around her waist, propelling
r onto the pile of possessions a split second before the
xt blistering volley rang out.

"What are you—?" Heather squealed in astonish-
ent, only to have her outcry smothered by the rending
d shattering of wood as multiple slugs drilled through
e sides of the wagon.

Davy held her down, an arm over both their heads.
utside, a man was roaring in what sounded like En-
ish, but Davy could not quite make out the words.
ullets stopped striking the bed. "Stay down," he di-
cted Heather, and snaked to the gate to see what was
ppening.

More Kanzas were down. The warriors were rallying,
ough. Those who had been in their lodges burst into
e open with arrows notched to bows. A flight of arrows
hizzed into the trees, and a shriek showed that at least
ie shaft scored.

Foremost among the defenders was White Feather,
nspicuous in his red blanket. At his direction, the Kan-
is formed a skirmish line, firing as swiftly as they could

unleash their shafts. Thick as a swarm of bees, the ar
rows zinged into the growth. The firing of the attacker
dwindled, as if the barrage was having an effect. Bu
then, when White Feather gestured and the warriors ad
vanced, another volley erupted, only this time it cam
from the north, not the east.

Davy divined the awful truth in a flash of insight. Th
raiders had split their force, positioning half to the north
to catch the defenders at just the right moment. In horro
he saw the Kanzas go down, fully half of the warrior
writhing in torment or lying lifeless. Scarlet bloo
pumped from gaping wounds. Shattered faces and rup
tured torsos testified to the marksmanship of the attack
ers.

The Kanzas wavered. White Feather valiantly tried t
rally them, but many bolted for their lodges and the
families.

It was then that a great yell was heard, coming from
the woods. The language was Kanzan, spoken awk
wardly, Davy noticed, as if the man who spoke it wa
not all that proficient. But proficient enough. Whateve
was said had an effect. The warriors stopped milling an
glanced at one another in confusion. White Feather face
the woods and responded.

From out of the bushes stepped a short, thick man i
buckskins. Bearded and grungy, he wore a floppy ha
and held a Hawken rifle. Smirking devilishly, he ex
changed words with White Feather, whose countenanc
grew dour. Finally, the chief turned to his warriors an
issued commands in a strained tone.

Davy was flabbergasted when, one by one by one, th
Kanzas cast down their bows and discarded their quiv
ers. Knives and war clubs were also put aside.

No sooner were the defenders unarmed than figure

aterialized among the tree trunks. About thirty of them, Davy's quick count. Half to the east, half to the north. ifles leveled, they closed on the village, halting at the rimeter.

Next to the stocky man in the floppy hat was a tall, oad-shouldered individual who wore city clothes; a ack suit, frilly white shirt, cloak, and silk hat. He oked as out of place there in the wilderness as the ocky frontiersman would look at an opera.

Yet no one would dare point it out or laugh at him, r the tall man radiated a potent presence, a force of ill, so to speak, that set him apart from ordinary men.

Leonine head held high, hands resting on the silver-laid butts of expensive flintlocks tucked under the fin-st leather belt money could purchase, the tall man tered the village, and strode up to White Feather. The ocky frontiersman tagged along, a hyena in the wake f a lion.

White Feather squared his shoulders. Though de-ated, his tribesmen wounded or dead on all sides, omen and children pleading pitiably for aid, he jutted s chin in bold defiance.

The tall man stopped. In a voice that boomed like a rass bell, he said to his stocky companion. "Tell this retch, Rickert, that no more of his people will be armed if they do exactly as I say."

"Yes, sir, Mr. Dugan, sir," Rickert answered meekly. e opened his mouth, but Dugan touched his shoulder.

"I wasn't done, cretin. Also inform these vermin that ey will provide food and drink for my entire company, ithout complaint. After they have tended to their ounded, of course. We're not heartless savages like ey are, after all."

"I understand, sir."

119

White Feather listened impassively, then replied Rickert translated as the chief went along. "He says tha his people will do whatever we want. He begs us not t hurt any more of them." White Feather paused and sur veyed the slaughter. "He asks why we did this? He wants to know what his people ever did to us that w should cut them down without mercy? He says, wha manner of men are we that we can shoot unarme women and children? That we can—"

"Enough!" Alexander Dugan snapped, slicing the ai with a gloved hand. "Who is this heathen to questio *my* motives? Instruct him to see to those who were hur But he is to stay with us at all times. One wrong mov by any of his followers, and you are to kill him—in stantly. Be sure the cur comprehends."

"White Feather, sir."

"What?"

"His name is White Feather."

"As if I care," Dugan said, and brushing past th chief, he stalked toward the wagon. Half a dozen me flanked him, protecting him. Some wore buckskins. Oth ers wore the garb of river rats. Among the latter wa Benchley.

Davy was going to rise up and show himself whe fingers clutched his arm. Heather was quaking, he lovely face as white as a sheet.

"He's found us! Oh, God! Shoot him, Davy! Shoo now, before he sees us! While you still can!"

The Tennessean balked at the notion of shooting any one—even a butcher like Dugan—from ambush. He ha never killed an enemy who did not have a chance t defend himself. It went against his grain.

"Oh, hell!" Heather cried, and tearing Liz fro

Davy's hand, she heaved up, taking aim at her stepfather, who stopped abruptly, eyes widening.

The men with Dugan reacted on impulse, elevating their own guns to cut Heather down. Davy lunged, batting the rifle aside with one hand while throwing his other arm around her and pinning her to the side of the wagon.

"No!" Heather protested. "Let me go! He must be stopped! You don't know what you're doing!"

"I'm saving you from being killed," Davy said, but it was no use. She kicked and battered him, seeking to break free.

Alexander Dugan composed himself and came on, a jerk of his arm sufficient to have his men lower their rifles. Smugly, he said, "Quit struggling, my dear. The fellow has done you a tremendous favor."

Under the wagon, Flavius Harris had his own hands full. He had been holding Becky close the whole time, shielding her with his own body. When she heard her mother's shout, she tried to cry out and scramble past the rear wheel. Flavius clamped a hand over her mouth and would not let go. Into her ear, he whispered, "Be still, girl. They might not spot us under here."

It was just possible. The wagon was wide enough that unless someone hunkered and peeked underneath, they'd escape notice.

Above them, Davy Crockett had taken Liz from Heather. Immediately, he was covered by the cutthroats who accompanied Dugan. Holding the rifle by the stock and the barrel, Davy carefully lowered it, leaning it against the wagon, well out of Heather's reach.

Alexander Dugan wore an enigmatic smile. "I've always admired men with intelligence. It's a mark of greatness when a person keeps their wits about them in a crisis." He stepped to the wagon. "I should know. I always keep mine about me."

Davy decided then and there that Alexander Dugan was as full of himself as a balloon was full of hot air. Any fuller, and Dugan might well burst at the seams.

Suddenly Benchley glided forward and said over Dugan's shoulder, "That's him, sir."

"To whom are you referring, Rufus?"

"That guy, there," Benchley said, pointing at Davy. "He's the bastard I told you about, the one who killed Sontag."

Dugan's dark smoldering eyes focused on the Tennessean. "Do tell. Well, we will resolve that issue later. Right this minute, I want to see my granddaughter. Where is she, Heather?"

Under the wagon, Becky attempted once again to slip from Flavius's grasp. She was an eel, slippery and clever, and it was all Flavius could do to hold on.

Davy was holding his hands out from his sides, making no attempt to unlimber his pistols. Benchley eyed him as if he were a piglet fit for butchering; the river rat wanted revenge for Sontag, Davy guessed.

"I'm waiting," Alexander Dugan said when Heather did not respond promptly.

"I don't know where she is, damn you." Leaning down, she shook a fist at him. "Did you ever stop to think that one of *us* might have been hit when you fired on these poor, peaceful Indians? Isn't it bad enough that Jon may never fully recover from the other day?"

"The other day? What are you talking about?"

Heather lanced a thumb at Benchley. "Rufus and his friends. They opened fire on us. Nearly killed Becky and me. Jon took a bullet." Her words were choked off by commingled rage and sorrow. Coughing, she spat, "I knew you were a monster, Alex. But I never figured you would stoop so low as to endanger Becky.''

Alexander Dugan flushed. His craggy features as flinty as quartz, he pivoted. ''Is this true, Rufus? You fired on them after I gave specific instructions to the contrary?''

Rufus Benchley's Adam's apple bobbed. ''Hamlin fired on us first, Mr. Dugan.'' He shrugged. ''Besides, we aimed high so as not to hit anyone. All we wanted was to scare Hamlin into turning Heather and the girl over, like you ordered.''

Dugan's hand lashed out and clamped on the river rat's chin. Thick fingers squeezed. Although Benchley was bigger and broader, he gulped and did not lift a hand to protect himself.

''Rufus, Rufus, Rufus,'' Dugan said, in the manner of a parent scolding an overzealous child. ''How many times must I make myself clear? My directions are always to be carried out to the letter. When I told you that I did not want you to open fire on the wagon, *I damn well meant it*.''

Alexander Dugan had to be immensely strong. With a short flick of his arm, he threw Benchley to the ground. A pistol sprang into his hand. Cocking it, Dugan pointed the weapon at the river rat's face, the muzzle nearly brushing the tip of Benchley's wide nose.

Benchley froze, petrified. A tiny squeak escaped him and his hands trembled uncontrollably. The other men held their collective breath, not one rash enough to interfere.

Slowly, the redness in Dugan's features faded. Pursing his lips, he let the hammer down and jammed the pistol back under his elaborately tooled belt. ''Never let it be said that Alexander Dugan can't be merciful,'' he announced. ''You've been a competent, loyal employee for many years now, Rufus. This is the first time you've ever let me down.''

"True.'' Benchley grasped at the straw. "Honest, boss. I'm sorry for the mistake. I was only trying to get them back for you, to make you happy.''

Like someone patting a dog that had earned a bone, Alexander Dugan patted the bearish river rat's head. "Relax, Rufus. No real harm was done. In fact, you've done me a marvelous service.'' Dugan faced Heather. "Is there any prospect of Hamlin dying?'' he asked hopefully.

Heather was out of the wagon before anyone could think to stop her. Fingernails bared, she tore into her stepfather, a female fury gone berserk. Her first swing raked his cheek. Then Dugan grasped her wrists, holding her at arm's length until her struggles ceased.

"There, now. Is the childishness out of your system?'' Dugan pushed her against the wagon, straightened, and smoothed his jacket and cloak. "Honestly, Heather. There are times when you act half your age.''

Heather sagged, defeated, tears streaking her cheeks. "You miserable son of a bitch.''

"Is that any way for lady to talk?'' Dugan rose onto the tips of his toes to see into the wagon. Studying Hamlin, he said offhandedly, "He was hit in the head? How bad is it?''

Davy answered. "He's blind.''

"You don't say?''

"The Kanzas have helped us treat him, but he's shown no sign of improvement.''

Over the years, Davy had learned that sometimes a single act or expression could reveal a lot about a person. Alexander Dugan's next act disclosed all there was worth knowing about the most powerful man in St.

Louis. It bared his true nature to the world. It illuminated the vile depths of wickedness to which human beings could sink: Alexander Dugan smiled.

"How fitting. He tried to steal my granddaughter from me, and fate repaid him. Justice has been served."

Heather heaved upright. "*Justice?* Was it just of you to forbid me to see Jon? Was it just of you to threaten to take me to court if I didn't obey?"

Dugan was unaffected by her outburst. "I didn't merely threaten, my dear. As you'll recall, I carried through on my *promise*. It's the reason I'm here. You defied me. You defied the judge. You defied the law. Blame yourself, if you must blame anyone. Hamlin's condition is on your shoulders, not mine."

Heather coiled as if to tear into him again. With a lithe bound, Davy Crockett vaulted from the wagon and landed in front of her just as she pounced. He held her back, braced for a frenzy. Instead, Heather collapsed against him, sobbing pitiably.

Alexander Dugan sniffed, then commanded, "My granddaughter! Find her, gentlemen! Half of you search the village. The other half keep an eye on the heathens. Be quick about it!"

Dugan's lieutenants, Benchley and Rickert, barked orders, dividing the men. Benchley's half stood guard while Rickert's bunch fanned out to poke their heads into every lodge and check behind every tree.

This whole time, the Kanzas had been ministering to the wounded and carrying the dead to a grassy tract adjacent to the river. Grief-stricken wails and shrieks rose in a steady, mournful chorus. Dogs had come out of hiding to lap at puddles of blood. One brazen canine commenced chewing on the corpse of a young woman. Her husband sprang on it with flying fists and pummeled it so severely that when it finally slid out of his grasp, blood poured from its mouth and nostrils. It staggered eight or nine yards, then keeled over.

White Feather was misery personified. Heartbroken by the suffering of his people, he stood with head bowed, shoulders slumped.

Alexander Dugan was unmoved by the carnage. Arms folded, he surveyed the scene without a hint of emotion.

When a woman who had been shot in the stomach writhed in the arms of those seeking to help her, and screamed so shrilly that the short hairs on Davy's neck prickled, Alexander Dugan did not bat an eye.

When a warrior whose jaw had been blown off stumbled past, Alexander Dugan gazed at the Kanza in cold disdain.

When a little girl who had part of her leg shot away was borne past in the arms of her mother, Alexander Dugan stepped back so the blood dripping from the girl would not splatter his polished boots.

Davy had never met anyone quite like him before. Dugan held himself aloof from the rest of the world, as if he were superior to the vast majority of humankind and all lesser beings were beneath his notice.

The Tennessean could not help himself. "Don't you care?" he blurted.

"About what, pray tell?"

Davy encompassed the village with a sweep of an arm. "The bloodshed. The anguish you've caused."

"They're Indians," Dugan said, as if that justified the deed.

"Indians are people, too."

Alexander Dugan laughed gustily. "I overestimated your intelligence, it appears. Heathens are scum. Cattle, if you will. Stamping them out is the same as stamping on ants, or crushing maggots. It's not worth troubling the conscience about.''

Heather stopped weeping. Dabbing at her eyes, she said bitterly, "Save your breath, Davy. My dear stepfather has a heart of ice, if he has a heart at all."

"Oh, come now," Dugan said. "Were I as callous as you claim, would I be so concerned about the welfare of my granddaughter?"

"Concerned?" Brittle scorn laced Heather's tone. "All you care about is yourself. You want to take her from me to punish me for not living my life as *you* see fit."

"Let's not get into that again."

Heather was on the verge of tears. "If only I were a man!" she snarled.

"It would be easier all around," Dugan conceded. "A man would know better than to wed below his station. First you married that fool, Tom Fitzgerald. Then after he died, you fell for a worthless specimen like Jonathan Hamlin. Detect a trend?"

It was the proverbial straw that broke the camel's back. Or, in this case, Heather's self-control. Venting a low, bestial growl, she threw herself at her stepfather. This time Davy was not quite fast enough. She clawed at Dugan's eyes, at his neck. Dugan was driven backward, caught off-balance. Fortunately for him, Benchley and two others sprang to his defense and seized her.

Red streaks marred Dugan's cheeks. Touching a forefinger to a furrow, he stared at the blood on his fingertip. "Any vestige of feeling I had for you, girl, is now gone. May God forgive you, because I never will."

"I'm not a *girl*," Heather raged. "I'm a *woman*! And I can live my life as I want."

Under the wagon, Becky had stopped struggling. Flavius relaxed his grip, but he did not release her, just in case. From their vantage point, he could see booted feet moving briskly about the village, going from hut to hut. So far no one had thought to check the shadows under the wagon.

From inside the wagon came a loud groan. Davy heard movement, and a thump. He was turning to investigate when the blanket parted.

Jonathan Hamlin was ghostly pale. Hands propped against the side, he stared outward. "Heather?" he croaked. "What's happening? Are you all right?"

Alexander Dugan snickered. "Lazarus rises. It's too bad you've lost your vision, Hamlin. You can't appreciate how pathetic you look."

"Dugan!" Jonathan gasped and took a step forward. Unknown to him, he was inches from the loading gate. He tripped and fell.

Davy tried to catch him, but succeeded only in snatching Jonathan's arm. Hamlin crashed onto the ground and lay stunned, his mouth working silently.

"Jon!" Heather screeched.

Spurred by her shout, Jonathan attempted to rise, but he was much too weak.

Chuckling, Alexander Dugan squatted and placed a single finger on Jonathan's back, holding him down. "Pitiful. Why my stepdaughter has always been attracted to weaklings, I will never know." Cuffing Jonathan lightly on the temple, Dugan began to rise, then paused, his gaze drifting under the wagon. Triumph lit his features.

"My, my. What do we have here?"

Chapter Ten

"I hate this," Flavius Harris declared. When it did not elicit a response, he said it again, only louder. "I can't tell you how much I hate this."

Davy Crockett sighed. They were bound at the wrists and ankles, lying in the gloom of a small Kanza lodge. They had been there for a couple of hours, by Davy's reckoning. His legs were stiff and cramped, his forearms nearly numb. He wriggled them every so often to keep the circulation going, but it was a losing proposition. Benchley had taken perverse delight in tying the ropes especially tight.

"This is a fine how-do-you-do," Flavius lamented. Just when his hopes had been raised that they would soon return to their canoe, everything had gone to hell in spectacular fashion.

"It's not as if I planned it this way."

"I'm not blaming you personally," Flavius said.

"The Lord knows, you were only doing what you thought was right."

Davy could not be certain whether a note of biting sarcasm underlay the statement. "Crying over spilt milk won't get us anywhere. We need to get free."

"No fooling?" Flavius said, and laughed without warmth. "What I wouldn't give for the chance to wrap my hands around that high-and-mighty bastard's throat! Just like he did to me!"

It had happened after Alexander Dugan discovered Flavius and Becky. At gunpoint, they had been ordered to crawl out. Becky had tried to go to her mother, but Dugan swept her into his arms and gave the girl a big hug. She had to break loose, calling him mean. When Dugan held her at arm's length and gave her a rough shake, Flavius had gone to her aid.

He should have thought twice. It had earned him a rifle stock in the gut, courtesy of Benchley. And while he writhed and sputtered on the ground, Alexander Dugan had towered over him. Fingers made of ironwood locked on his throat. He had been lifted as if he were an infant.

Dugan's eyes had blazed into his. "And who might you be, fat man?" he had snarled. "No. Let me guess. You're another *meddler*. Another fool who doesn't know his place."

Flavius could not have answered if his life depended on it. He had scarcely been able to breathe, and the world around him had spun dizzily.

"Don't hurt him!" Becky had cried. "He's my friend."

Flavius was convinced her appeal had saved his life; there had been murder in Dugan's blazing eyes.

Now Davy shifted to relieve a cramp in his left leg. "It's been awful quiet outside," he said.

Initially, loud weeping and singsong laments had risen in a mournful dirge as the Kanzas grieved for the fallen. Apparently, their highly vocal sorrow had grated on Alexander Dugan's nerves. Dugan had hollered at them to quiet down—or else. Rickert translated, and the level of sound had dropped off. But total silence had not descended until a short while ago.

"I wonder what Lucifer is up to," Flavius said.

Raw worry ate at Davy's innards. Worry for Heather and Becky, for Hamlin, and for the poor Kanzas, whose kindness had reaped tragedy on a terrible scale. Fully one-third of the band had been slain or severely wounded.

A shadow filled the opening. Into the lodge came two burly cutthroats in buckskins. They cut the ropes that bound the Tennesseans' ankles, brusquely hauled them erect, and shoved them through the opening.

Tottering, Davy blinked in the bright sunlight. His legs were sluggish, hardly able to support his weight. A rifle barrel gouged hard into his spine and pain seared from his hips to his neck.

"Move it, mister. The boss wants to see you."

Flavius was worse off. His legs would not support him. Again and again he attempted to stand and always his knees buckled. He was kicked and jabbed and slapped until, in indignation, he fumed, "Do you think I'm doing this on purpose? You're the ones who tied the rope too damned tight!"

One of the men yelled. Two more appeared. Flavius was hoisted up and propelled none too gently toward the wagon.

Alexander Dugan was seated on a log that had been

dragged into the village just for him. On his right was Heather, downcast. On his left was Becky, streaks from dried tears staining her cheeks. Ten or so of Benchley's men stood in a group, waiting. The rest ringed the Kanzas, who were huddled to one side, many bandaged, some groaning and moaning. Of Jonathan Hamlin, there was no sign.

Davy was pushed violently. Stumbling to his knees in front of Dugan, he slowly unfurled and matched Dugan's icy stare. "It must be nice, thinking you're God."

Benchley and some of the others glanced at their employer as if expecting him to lash out. Alexander Dugan surprised them.

"I would keep a civil tongue were I you, Mr. Crockett. I'm inclined to be merciful. My stepdaughter has told me what you did. How you tracked them all the way from the Mississippi because you were worried about the dangers they would encounter. Quite remarkable, if true."

Flavius took offense at the implication. "Oh, it's true, all right. I tried to talk him out of it, but he can be a stubborn cuss once he's put his mind to something."

Dugan's brow knit. "Does your friend always go around doing good deeds, Mr. Harris?"

"It's sort of his life's work."

"Amazing," Dugan said, and smirked at Davy. "Haven't you heard, Mr. Crockett? Living by the golden rule will make a martyr of you." Dugan idly brushed at a speck of dust on his sleeve. "As for my presuming to act like the Almighty, I remind you that great wealth offers certain rewards. Among them is great power. I have senators and congressmen at my beck and call. The ear of the president is mine whenever I need to speak with him." His chest swelled. "I can do whatever I want, whenever I want. With impunity."

"Are you trying to impress me?" Davy said. "You're wasting your breath. I generally hold a low opinion of polecats who grind blind people into the dirt." Davy gazed at the bodies lined up near the river. Crows and buzzards had gathered, but were keeping their distance for the time being, hungrily watching from the trees. "To say nothing of butchers who slaughter women and kids."

"I do what I have to, and make apologies to no one," Dugan said sternly.

Heather stirred and sneered. "That's right, Davy. He's perfect. He doesn't ever need to say he's sorry because he never does anything wrong."

"You're catching on at last," her stepfather said. "And speaking of apologies, I trust you will have one to offer the judge when you're hauled before him?"

"What judge?" Davy asked.

"Didn't she tell you?" Dugan leaned back. "I took her to court, Mr. Crockett. It was my contention that she is an unfit mother. That she has no business rearing Rebecca. And the judge agreed. He awarded custody of Becky to me." He paused. "But Heather and Hamlin whisked her away. Evidently they had the whole thing planned out in advance, in case she lost the case. Hamlin had a wagon waiting, stocked with supplies. But I wasn't about to let them steal Becky away from me."

"Wait a minute," Davy said. "Heather is a fine mother. How could you get away with claiming otherwise?"

"Fine, is she?" Alexander Dugan bestowed a look of sheer contempt on his stepdaughter. "Perhaps I should tell you the whole story."

Davy looked at Heather, who averted her face as if in shame.

"The truth of the matter, Southerner, is that Heather has always been headstrong. Even as a little girl. Whenever I would ask her to do something she didn't want to do, such as tidying up her room, she would say that I had no right, that I wasn't her real father."

"A lot of children go through a rebellious spell," Davy said, thinking of the years he had been on his own after he ran away from home.

"Hers wasn't a *spell*," Dugan said. "When she grew into young womanhood, she became worse. She always had to do things her way." He counted off her faults on his fingers. "She associated with the wrong people. She stayed out to all hours of the night. She visited establishments no self-respecting lady ever would."

Heather turned. "It was only a year or so. I stopped when I came to my senses."

"Too late, I'm sorry to say. By then you had met Tom Fitzgerald. A man with little schooling and no social standing. As I recall, he had about a hundred dollars to his name when the two of you wed."

"I loved him."

"Love doesn't put food on the table or keep you clothed on a cold night." Alexander Dugan frowned. "It wouldn't have hurt you to show an interest in some of the men I preferred."

Tingling had developed in Davy's forearms, followed by pain. His blood was flowing again. He flexed both arms a few times, remarking, "If you felt that way, why did you give her husband a job?"

"You know about that?" Dugan dismissed his act of kindness with a gesture. "I had to do something. Fitzgerald was always talking about going off to New York or Philadelphia or somewhere or other to make his fortune. A typical dreamer.''

Davy understood. ''You gave him the job so he wouldn't leave St. Louis?''

''Precisely. I paid that fool twice the going rate.'' Dugan put a hand on Becky's shoulder. ''I would do anything to keep Rebecca near me.''

''And Hamlin?''

Alexander Dugan's lip curled in disgust. ''What needs to be said? He's worse than Fitzgerald, if that's possible. The man is an *accountant*, for crying out loud. What kind of life could he give them?''

Heather was growing angry. ''Jon loves me,'' she declared.

''There you go again. Love is vastly overrated.''

Davy gave voice to the question uppermost in his mind. ''So what now?''

''What now, indeed?'' Dugan rose and scrutinized the assembled Kanzas. ''I doubt that those pathetic scum will give me any more trouble. Neither will Hamlin. Heather can raise a fuss all she wants after we get back, but the judge has ruled in my favor and there is nothing she can do about it.'' Dugan stared down at Davy and rested a hand on a pistol. ''That leaves you and your partner.''

Flavius did not like the thinly veiled threat. ''We're no danger to you. Let us go our own way and that'll be the end of it. No hard feelings.''

Dugan rubbed his chin. ''If only I could be certain . . .''

''You can!'' Flavius said. ''Why should we care what you do? All we ever wanted to do was help out. We didn't know about the judge, about you having custody.

135

So just let us go on our way and everyone will be happy all around.''

Benchley took a half step forward. "What about Sontag, Mr. Dugan? They have to answer for him, don't they? He was a good man, after all.''

"Yes, he was," Alexander Dugan agreed. Clasping his hands behind his broad back, he paced in front of Davy. "I always stick up for my employees, Mr. Crockett. Harm one and you answer to me. I realize there are extenuating circumstances here. You were only protecting Heather and Becky. But that does not excuse what you did.''

"He was trying to kill me," Davy explained. "You would have done the same.''

"Possibly. Probably, even," Dugan admitted. "But I'm not you and you're not me. I must satisfy my men that justice has been done.''

Heather jumped erect. "Harm a hair on his head, and I swear that I'll see you punished.''

Dugan made as if to slap her, but did not. "You try my patience, woman. Who would you go to? There is no law west of the Mississippi. Out here, we make our own.''

Benchley aimed his rifle at Davy. The click of the hammer was unnaturally loud. "Just say the word, Mr. Dugan, and I'll send this bastard into the hereafter.''

"Why waste a bullet?" Alexander Dugan said. "Apply your imagination, Rufus.''

"Sir?''

"Bring him away. Mr. Harris, also. And the log that I was sitting on." Dugan walked away. "Not my stepdaughter or Rebecca, though. They must stay here.''

Heather took a few steps towards him but Rickert

seized her, holding her wrists. "What are you planning to do?" she demanded.

"Make an object lesson of him," Alexander Dugan said.

Davy was gripped by a pair of burly men who half dragged, half carried him northward. Four others brought the log. He was at a loss to explain what Dugan was up to until he saw where they were headed. Digging in his heels, he sought to free himself. But the pair of underlings were not to be denied. One got behind him and applied a stout shoulder to his back while the other pulled him by the elbows.

They filed past the slain Kanza. A warrior gaped blankly skyward. Curled in a fetal position was a young woman who had been heavy with child. In another spot lay a girl of five or six, her features oddly serene.

Alexander Dugan halted at the edge of the river and declared, "This will do nicely."

Flavius was thoroughly confounded. For a minute he thought the man intended to throw Davy in. Then Dugan commanded that the log be rolled into the water and held fast so that it could not drift down the river.

"Bring rope," Dugan added.

Comprehension filled Flavius with dread. "You can't!" he said. He was helpless to intervene, though. For when he tried, one of the men who had seized him sharply twisted both arms.

"Behave yourself, Mr. Harris," Alexander Dugan said, "or you'll be accorded the same treatment. As it is, I'm only sparing your life because I need someone to drive the wagon."

Davy was pushed toward the log. He resisted strenuously, forcing more men to lend a hand. They lifted him bodily, positioned him over the log, and lowered him so he lay on top of it, faceup.

The short pieces of rope binding his wrists were untied. His arms were roughly jerked back and down, flush with the rough bark, and the same with his legs. In moments, he had been bound again, this time by longer ropes that were fed underneath the log to link both wrists and both ankles.

Benchley tittered as he finished tying. Poking Davy in the ribs, he said, "This ought to give you plenty of time to regret what you did. Sontag was a good friend of mine."

Alexander Dugan stepped closer and grinned. "This river isn't very wide or very deep, but it should suffice." He pushed on the log, making it bob. "The trick will be to hold your breath long enough."

Davy had nothing to lose by saying, "If I get out of this alive, I'm coming for you. You've crossed the line one too many times."

"What line?" Dugan bantered. Pushing harder, he chuckled when the log dipped and water rose as high as Davy's waist. "Be thankful for the few extra minutes of life I've granted by not having you shot."

From the wagon rose a strident shout, "Alex! For the love of God! No!"

"Please, grandpa!" Becky added.

"Females," Dugan said wearily, and stepped to the end of the log. Bending, he placed both hands flat. "It has been interesting," he said. "Keep in mind that I bear you no personal malice. What I do, I do because my men expect it of me."

Fear welled up in Flavius. The Irishman was the best friend he'd ever had, as dear if not dearer to him than his own brothers. Besides that, without Davy he stood as much chance of surviving to reach Tennessee as a snowflake had in an inferno.

Suddenly ramming his shoulders into the men holding him, Flavius launched himself at the log. He had no clear idea of what he would do, should he reach it. He only knew he must stop Dugan. But he had taken just three steps when a leg caught him across the shins. Down he crashed. As he rose, fingers entwined in his hair. Others clamped onto his shoulders and neck.

"Enough of that, Mr. Harris," Dugan warned. "Unless you would rather I had another log brought over?"

Davy glanced at his friend. "Do as he wants. I'll be fine."

"Think so?" Dugan said. To emphasize his point, he pushed the log out toward the middle of the river. In moments the current caught hold and it hurtled eastward.

"Nooooooo!" Heather screamed.

Davy twisted for a last glimpse of the village. It was an error on his part. The movement upset his critical balance on the log. It rolled, rushing him toward the water. He had a mere heartbeat to suck air into his lungs, then he plunged under the surface. The chill water blurred his vision and seeped into his nose, into his ears.

Davy gagged. He could not help himself. Air gushed from his mouth, water gushed in. In trying to expel it, he swallowed more. It filled his mouth, his throat. Unable to control himself, he coughed, which allowed in even more.

He was drowning. Davy struggled to turn the log, throwing his shoulders and hips into a right-hand spin, hoping it would add to the momentum of the log's turn. It did. The log spun up and around, raising him out of the river.

Sunlight splashed his face. Water spewed from his

mouth. Davy broke into a fit of coughing. Almost too late, he realized that the log was going into another turn.

Davy tensed his arms and legs so the ropes were pulled tight, then froze. The log steadied, with him on top. He had gained a respite, but for how long?

Davy gingerly craned his neck for a look behind him. The village was already gone. The log had sailed around a bend and was on a long straight stretch. Did he hear faint mocking laughter, or was it his imagination?

The log bounced and swayed. So long as it did not spin, he would be safe. But he soon learned that whenever it hit a submerged rock or another obstacle, it tilted erratically and begin to rotate in either direction, depending on the angle.

He had to counteract the effect by tugging on the ropes in the opposite direction, which in itself entailed risk. Because if he tugged too hard, then the log would roll completely over, submerging him again.

His only hope was to free himself. The only problem was that any movement on his part, however slight, would also set the log to spinning. He was damned no matter what he did.

Willing himself not to panic, Davy tentatively tested the loops binding his wrists by lifting both arms and pulling. He thought that if he applied equal pressure to both ends at the same time, it would have no effect on the log.

He was wrong. It lurched to the left. Davy attempted to right it, but gravity worked against him. He saw the water rush at his face and took a deep breath before he went under. This time only a little got into his mouth and nose. Marshaling his strength, he heaved to the right.

As before, the log rotated, raising him up out of the river. As before, he stopped it when he was directly on top. Relaxing, he racked his brain for a means of breaking his bonds without perishing.

Davy heard bubbling sounds. The current was going faster. So was the log. It barreled into another bend, careened off a large rock or boulder, then canted wildly back and forth. Davy surged against the ropes, first in one direction, then another. His left arm slipped under. The log rolled upward, though, sparing him. When it steadied, he exhaled.

He could not go on like this for very long. Something had to be done. Beaching the log was his best bet, but how to do it when he couldn't steer? Or could he?

Carefully shifting, Davy peered ahead. The river was ten to fifteen feet wide on average. To reach either shore he must divert the log at a sharp angle. Holding his breath, he tried by wrenching on his legs, not his arms. The log moved, but not as he wanted. Instead of slanting toward the north shore, it rotated again.

Swirling water enclosed him. Davy heaved to right himself, but nothing happened. He heaved again, in vain. Anxious that he was taking too long, Davy threw himself against his restraints. He sensed that the log was traveling sideways instead of end-on, as it had been. Something had gone dreadfully wrong.

Davy exerted every ounce of strength in his body. He might as well have tried to upend the moon. Muscles bunched, he surged to the right, then to the left. His lungs were in torment, his throat ached. He could not last much longer.

That was when the log was jolted by a jarring impact. Davy's breath whooshed out, water whooshed in. Gagging, he braced for the end. Another impact sent the log lurching upward. Air brushed his face, and he heard a grating noise. When he blinked and cleared his eyes, he saw that the log had come to ground on the south shore, on the tip of a gravel bar. He was safe!

A new sound was the first inkling Davy had that his thinking was premature. A rumbling grunt warned him he was not alone.

Lumbering toward the log was a shaggy grizzly.

Chapter Eleven

Flavius Harris was shattered. He stared after the log bearing his best friend until a bend hid it from view. The laughter of Benchley and some of the others barely registered. Too dazed to resist, he was hauled from the river to the wagon.

When Rickert produced a Green River knife and sawed at the rope that bound his wrists, Flavius stirred to life. He girded himself to bolt past Dugan's cutthroats and make for the woods. If he could shake them, he would follow the river eastward in the hope of saving Davy.

His plan was foiled when Benchley shoved a pistol against his ribs and snapped, "Climb on the wagon, mister. You're driving, remember?"

"What?" Flavius said, confused. Then he remembered Dugan's comment earlier. A jab of the flintlock goaded him into obeying.

The oxen were being hitched. Hoofs clopped as some

of Dugan's bunch led horses from the trees. The big man himself escorted Heather and Becky to the rear of the wagon. Twisting, Flavius saw everything.

"Up you go, my dear," Dugan said, offering a hand to his stepdaughter.

Heather slapped it aside. "What if I refuse?"

"I will leave you here with your Indian hosts. And you will never see Rebecca again." Sliding his hands under Becky's arms, Dugan swung her up and over the loading gate. "So what will it be?"

"God, how I despise you," Heather said. Defeated, she joined her daughter.

A low groan from within drew Flavius around. Jonathan Hamlin was lying on the left-hand side. Dugan's men must have thrown him in when Flavius wasn't looking. Heather and Becky scurried to turn him over and cover him with a blanket.

Flavius turned just as Alexander Dugan walked by. "You're taking Hamlin back too?" he said in surprise.

Dugan paused. "Of course. If I left him here with the savages, they might take him under their wing. Look out for him. Treat him as one of their own." Dugan's features contorted into a mask of hatred. "I want him to suffer, Mr. Harris. He helped kidnap my granddaughter, didn't he? A certain judge who owes me favors will see to it that Hamlin spends the rest of his days rotting in prison."

"But he's blind," Flavius said. "Hasn't he endured enough already?"

"Not by a long shot." Dugan flared his nostrils like a bull about to go on a rampage. "You have a forgiving nature, Mr. Harris. I don't. It probably won't surprise you to learn that I've made more than my share of enemies over the years. And the only reason none of them

chest and her arms wrapped around her legs. The girl had not uttered a word in hours. Flavius couldn't blame her. Just when the promise of a new life had brought joy to her heart, Alexander Dugan had brought her world crashing down around her.

"I heard what they were calling you," Heather said as Flavius hunkered. "They're animals. The whole lot of them."

Flavius glanced at the pair hovering close by. "Vultures is what they are," he said loudly. "No-account buzzards. Vermin who should be exterminated."

One of the men gripped his rifle as if to swing it and started to take a step, but the other man snagged his arm.

"Let it rest, Bly. He's just trying to provoke you. And remember our orders. Mr. Dugan doesn't want him touched. Not yet, anyhow."

Bly lowered the rifle, then sneered. "Our turn will come, Harris. It's no secret. Mr. Dugan has plans for you, mister. Plans that'll make you think your friend in the funny cap got off easy."

Becky stirred. "I wish they were all dead, mom! Every last one! Even grandpa!"

The girl's vehemence stunned Flavius almost as much as it did her mother. Heather put down the bowl and spoon. Moving to Becky, she placed an arm over her daughter's slender shoulders. "There, there. Everything will work out, sweetheart. I promise."

"Don't treat me like I'm five years old," Becky said. "And don't lie to me." She stifled a sob. "Grandpa says I'm going to be his, all his. That Jon is going to prison and you won't be allowed to see me anymore."

"He's bluffing," Heather said, but her expression and her tone belied the statement.

Tears moistened Becky's eyes. Throwing her arms around her mother, she cried softly.

Bly snickered.

Something snapped deep within Flavius. He was on his feet and whirling with no conscious thought of doing so. His balled fist smashed into Bly's smirking mouth.

The buckskin-clad cutthroat spilled onto his back, blood seeping from his pulped lower lip.

Fists cocked, Flavius closed in. He landed a solid right as Bly tried to rise, connected with another left to the ribs that doubled Bly over. Arms encircled him from behind, but Flavius would not be denied. A short jab to Bly's cheek opened it like a rotten melon.

Bly sank to his knees, groggy, sputtering. He groped for his knife.

Shouts and pounding feet buffeted Flavius's ears. Ignoring them, his temples hammering from the beat of his own hot blood, he sought to hit Bly again. But more arms wrapped around him. His wrists were clamped onto and held securely.

Flavius heard Heather yelling. Then Becky. He blinked, and discovered Benchley in front of him, about to bash out his brains with a rifle stock.

"Enough!"

Alexander Dugan strode onto the scene. Shoving Benchley aside, he wrapped his fingers in the front of Flavius's hunting shirt. "Do you have a death wish, fool? Is that it?"

From out of nowhere hurtled Becky. She tore into Dugan like one possessed, her small fists beating on his leg, on his stomach. Dugan was so astounded that he stood there gaping blankly. Releasing Flavius, he tried to seize Becky's arms, but Heather reached the girl first and pulled her back.

"Don't you touch her, bastard!"

Dugan's features twisted with outrage. His eyes seemed to bulge. "I've about had my fill," he growled. "Another incident like this, and I won't be held responsible for my actions."

"How convenient," Heather said, bating him. "But then, you've always been an expert at making excuses, at justifying your heinous acts."

"Damn you—" Dugan rasped, quaking from the intensity of his emotions.

Heather stepped in front of Becky and thrust her chin toward her stepfather. "Go ahead. Hit me. It's what you want to do. So what if I'm a woman?"

One of the cutthroats was too bloodthirsty for his own good. "Do it, boss," he urged. "Punch the bitch."

Thunder and lightning clouded Alexander Dugan's features. He swung around, planting a blow on the man's temple that felled him where he stood. "Anyone else have something to say?" he bellowed. When none of his men responded, he stormed off.

Benchley wagged a finger under Flavius's nose. "You get off easy this time, fat man. But don't give us grief again. Or else."

The ruffians drifted toward the fires. Heather clasped Becky, and both mother and daughter shed quiet tears.

For his part, Flavius Harris made up his mind not to go to the slaughter meekly. First chance he got, he was going to grab a weapon and go down fighting. He would take as many with him as he could. Maybe if he timed it right he could take Dugan down, too. That alone would make his death worthwhile.

Flavius smiled grimly.

Chapter Twelve

It was close to midnight when Davy Crockett parted a cluster of grass with both hands and studied the camp. He was only twenty yards from a bored sentry who leaned on a rifle, struggling to stay awake.

For the better part of an hour, Davy had been working his way from the rise, snaking across the prairie flat on his belly. When he had commenced his approach, only a handful of cutthroats were still up. The majority had turned in early to be rested for the long day of hard travel ahead.

In every outfit were a few individuals who never seemed to need much sleep, who would rather swap tall tales or play cards or whatnot until all hours. Dugan's small army was no exception. Rufus Benchley and five others had been rolling dice and sipping from a silver flask until just a short while ago.

At last, though, everyone other than the jackleg sentry and three other guards were sound asleep. Or so it appeared. Davy suspected that some of those who had turned in late had not yet dozed off, so he decided to wait a while before going in.

Three of the four fires had been allowed to die low. The fourth was maintained by the sentries, one of whom drifted over even as Davy watched to add fuel to the dwindling flames.

That fire posed a problem. It happened to be thirty feet from the wagon. Dancing light bathed the nearest side, enough to make whisking the captives to safety a doubly perilous proposition.

Davy would not let that deter him. He had to do it, and after fifteen minutes elapsed, he angled toward the picket line. Most of the horses were dozing. He did not give the oxen a second look, since they posed no threat. Only the horses would kick up a fuss if he was not especially careful.

It amazed Davy that Dugan had not seen fit to post a man at the string. Some Indians, like the Blackfeet and the Lakotas, were outstanding horse thieves. A few of them could slip into Dugan's camp and make off with every last animal without any of the whites being the wiser.

Arrogance would be Dugan's undoing. The man was too cocksure, too plain overconfident. Maybe it stemmed from being so wealthy and powerful. Or maybe Dugan's attitude had spurred him to *become* the man that he was.

Davy gave a toss of his head to dispel such musing. He had to buckle down, had to concentrate on what he was doing to the exclusion of all else. Senses primed, he circled eastward, well shy of the bored sentry, whose eyes were shut.

The other three guards were at cardinal compass points: to the east, to the south, and to the west. Vague inky silhouettes in the night, none paced or patrolled the perimeter, leading Davy to believe that they were just as tired as their companion—which worked in his favor.

The east end of the horse string was cloaked in darkness. Davy crawled to within a few feet of the foremost animal, then slowly rose, so as not to startle it into nickering or fidgeting. The sorrel never so much as raised its head.

Davy quickly untied it, and three others besides. As he turned to lead them off, further down the line a dun pricked its ears and uttered a low whinny.

Crouching, Davy surveyed the camp. None of the sleepers had stirred. The guard to the north continued to doze on his rifle. Those to the west and the south had not moved. But the man to the east had turned.

Davy fingered the hilt of the knife tucked under his belt. The bow and war club were lying in the grass, out of ready reach. He dropped lower when the east guard walked slowly forward, scanning the picket line.

Did the man suspect? The four horses Davy had released were bunched together slightly apart from the rest. It might strike the sentry as odd.

The guard kept on advancing. Davy could have cussed a blue streak. After crabbing backwards until he was on the other side of the animals, he rose into a crouch and palmed the bone hilt of the Kanza weapon.

Among the sleepers, someone snored loud enough to rouse the dead. Davy cast repeated glances at the sprawled forms, but nobody stirred.

Now the east sentry was near enough for his bushy beard and beaver hat to be apparent. This was no wet-behind-the-ears river rat. Buckskins and moccasins identified him as a frontiersman, a savvy badger not likely to make many mistakes. Rifle leveled, he slowed.

158

Blood Rage

Davy could tell the man was staring at the four horses he had untied. No gambler worthy of the name would give a shovelful of chicken tracks for his chances should the man let out with a holler. His sole hope was that the frontiersman would come closer still.

The man did. Whispering, "What's going on here, you dumb critters? How in tarnation did you get all tangled up like that?" the man walked right up to them.

Davy was ready. Spearing the cold steel upward between two of the horses, he buried the knife to the hilt in the sentry's chest. He struck in the blink of an eye, as slick as a peeled onion.

The guard had lowered his rifle. Now he attempted to bring it up, but he was dead on his feet. It was child's play for Davy to snatch it. He yanked his knife out as the sentry dropped to the ground.

All had gone well. Retrieving the rope, Davy rotated to get out of there while the getting was good. He would stash the horses, then return for Flavius and the others. By morning they would be miles away. Dugan would never catch them.

"Grover? Is that you?"

Davy drew up short and glanced back. Rufus Benchley had sat up. Hair disheveled, blinking drowsily, Dugan's right-hand man scratched an armpit.

"Didn't you hear me? What in the hell are you doing over there?"

A bluff was called for. Imitating the dead man's inflection and tone, Davy answered, "Everything's fine, Rufus. I was just checkin' on the critters."

Benchley sleepily nodded, yawned, and started to lie back down.

Davy did not dally. He had taken about half a dozen

steps when the crack of doom pealed in the strident challenge of someone he had overlooked.

"Hold it right there, mister! You ain't Grover!"

It was the north sentry, the one Davy had assumed was still dozing. The man was midway along the string, rifle wedged to a shoulder.

The shout brought many of the cutthroats up out of their blankets. In a rush, some made for the horses. Benchley was in the lead, completely awake, a pistol in each hand. In the gloom, he did not notice the body. Tripping over it, he stumbled but caught himself by grasping one of the animals for support. "You!" he roared on seeing Davy.

The jig was up. The Irishman lashed out, his fist smashing into Benchley's jaw. As the ruffian staggered backward, Davy bolted for the open prairie and safety. He paused just long enough to grab the rifle and the war club.

It proved to be his undoing.

From out of the darkness hurtled burly figures. Human battering rams slammed into him, burying him beneath an avalanche of smelly, sweaty, cussing foes. Davy connected with a right, but absorbed punches to his gut and cheek. For a brief instant, he thought that he might shake them off and escape.

"Hold him, you simpletons!"

Alexander Dugan's command was obeyed to the letter. Another four underlings piled on. Their combined weight was enough to pin Davy flatter than a pancake. Helpless, he submitted to having his arms seized and to being pawed erect. A vicious slap made his ears ring.

"Enough, Rufus," Dugan scolded.

"But he killed Grover," Benchley reported, pointing. "Let me skin the polecat alive."

Dugan looked and scowled. "That's two good men I've lost on your account, Mr. Crockett." Stepping in front of Davy, he clasped his hands behind his back. "I thought we had seen the last of you. How in the world did you manage to free yourself from that log?"

"A grizzly cut me loose."

Benchley snorted and flourished a knife. "Don't listen to his bull, boss. Just say the word, and I'll make you a new tobacco pouch out of his hide."

Dugan held a hand up, quieting his subordinate. "When I want your advice, Rufus, I will ask for it." Dugan gripped Davy's chin and turned Davy's head back and forth, as if studying a creature that mystified him. "You puzzle me, sir. Were you born under a lucky star, or are higher powers at work? It seems you merit more interest than I supposed."

"You've brought the bloodshed on yourself," Davy said. "Release me and the others and we'll go our separate ways with no hard feelings."

Dugan sighed. "Now you are being childish. And tedious. I hold the upper hand, and I have no intention of relinquishing it." Gesturing, he ordered, "Bind him, then toss him into the wagon with the rest. Rufus, double the guard. And see that Grover is buried."

"That's decent of you, boss."

"Decent, hell. I don't want the smell of blood to lure in bears or wolves."

Only Davy's wrists were bound. Four men propelled him to the wagon. Like a sack of grain, he was bundled over the loading gate and thrown inside, with no regard for his well-being. His elbow lanced with agony, and he hit his head on a plank.

"Pard? Is that you?" Flavius Harris asked in astonishment. A commotion outside had awakened him, but he was slow in regaining his full faculties. Exhaustion had the others in the grip of heavy slumber.

"None other," Davy said. Forcing a wan grin, he declared, "I've come to rescue you."

Flavius was so elated, he let out with a Cherokee war whoop. He regretted it when Becky screamed, and Heather and Jonathan Hamlin both sat bolt upright in a panic.

"Mom! Mom!" the girl cried. "Indians are on us!"

"No, no, no!" Flavius said. "It was me! Everything is fine! Crockett's here!"

"Davy?" Becky said, twisting. Scooting across the pile of possessions, she rested her forehead against the Irishman's arm. "Grandpa Dugan gloated that he killed you."

"He nearly did."

Heather rose onto her knees and came closer. The excitement on her features died, dismay taking its place. "You were our last hope. And now you're in the same boat we are." She stopped and sagged, her spirit broken. "Alex has won. We don't stand a prayer."

"Where there's life, there's hope," Davy intoned. Turning his back to Flavius, he wriggled his bound wrists. "Time's a wasting. Do me, then I'll do you."

Flavius glanced at the blanket over the opening. "Didn't they tell you? Dugan promised to shoot me in the leg if so much as one of us gets loose."

"Dog my cats," Davy said. "He aims to rub us out anyway. Wouldn't you rather go down fighting instead of trussed up like piglets waiting to be turned into a holiday dish?"

"Since you put it that way," Flavius said, chuckling. His friend always did have a flair for a colorful turn of words. And for the first time since the attack on the

Kanza village, he entertained the notion that they might actually survive.

The Irishman always had that effect on folks. Flavius had seen it that time Davy bolstered the morale of the starving troops who were slogging through treacherous swampland in search of the elusive Creeks. He'd seen it when Davy inspired the farmers not to give up on account of drought. And he'd been there when Davy helped rally the Chippewas during bloody battle.

But as Flavius soon learned, being fired up with enthusiasm was one thing. Being able to translate that enthusiasm into results, quite another.

Try as he might—and Lordy, *how* he tried—Flavius made little headway. For over an hour he pried at the knots with his nails, but to no avail. In desperation, he bent and applied his teeth, like a beaver to a tree. He gnawed until his gums and tongue were sore, but all he succeeded in doing was loosening one measly loop. "Who the hell tied you?" he said, straightening to soothe a kink in his lower back.

"Benchley."

"The man is a wizard. I can't get these undone for the life of me."

Jonathan Hamlin had laid back down, but Becky and Heather were still awake, waiting anxiously. "Let me try," the mother proposed.

"Why not use the axe head?" Becky asked innocently. "Jon cut some roots with it once. It would work."

Davy and Flavius both swung toward the corner. The implements were right where they had always been. Flavius could not help himself and swore in the presence of the females. Embarrassed, he apologized, saying,

"Bless me if'n I'm not as smart as a box of rocks. I plumb forgot."

The Tennesseans moved to the corner. Flavius gripped the long handle and tried to swivel the axe around so the edge of the head was at the right angle. But, bound as he was, the heavy handle was difficult to manipulate. It swung down and cracked Davy across the forearms.

"Maybe we should switch," Davy suggested. Taking the handle, he gingerly lowered the head until it rested on the thick ropes around Flavius's wrists. "Don't move. I wouldn't want to open a vein."

Eagerly, Davy sawed. And sawed. And sawed. Pausing, he bent to examine the rope. The axe had cut less than a quarter of an inch into the hemp. "I've had a run of bad luck before, but this is enough to swear a parson off the Bible."

"What's the matter now, pard?"

"It's as dull as a butter knife," Davy lamented.

"Jon's been meaning to sharpen all our tools, but he just hasn't had the time," Heather disclosed.

Davy resumed sawing. Every ten minutes or so he had to take a break. The pain in his wrists and shoulders became too much to bear.

Another hour went by. Davy was beginning to think he would still be at it when the sun came up, when abruptly the last of the loops parted and fell.

"You did it!" Flavius crowed, then wanted to smother himself for being such a fool. He listened for shouts and the drumming of feet, but no outcry was raised.

"Hurry," Davy urged. "My turn."

Even with the use of his fingers, it took some doing. Flavius finally loosened the Irishman's restraints, and did the same for Heather, her daughter, and Hamlin, who sat up as he finished.

"What will you do now?" Hamlin asked.

"Make a break for the horses," Davy answered. He reached for the hanging blanket.

"You'd never make it with me along. I'd be too much of a burden." Hamlin slid against the side, his knees pressed to his chest. "Go without me. I won't hold it against you."

Heather scrambled to her beloved. "Don't be silly. I could no more leave you than I could leave Becky. We're in this together. Just hold onto my hand and I'll guide you."

"I'd only get you killed," Hamlin persisted, launching the two into an emotional argument. Hamlin absolutely refused to endanger them, and Heather was equally insistent that he go.

Davy listened with half an ear while easing the blanket aside a few inches. The four horses he had untied were back on the string. But they were not what interested him the most. For standing a dozen feet from the wagon were two husky cutthroats, both wide awake and armed to the teeth.

A hunch motivated Davy to go to the front of the wagon and peek out. As he feared, two more of Dugan's men had been posted near the end of the tongue.

Heather and Hamlin continued to spat. Davy motioned, saying, "Save your breath. It'll be a long day in January before we can sneak off."

"What do you mean?" Jon asked.

Davy told them about the extra guards, ending with, "Dugan isn't the sort to make the same mistake twice. We're stuck here for certain sure."

Depression seized them. Flavius cradled his head in

his hands and wished he had listened to Matilda, for once, and not gone on the gallivant.

Becky timidly snuggled next to her mother, who sorrowfully stroked her hair, and Hamlin's.

Davy leaned his temple against the cloth cover and closed his eyes. To be frustrated now, after so much effort, was profoundly upsetting. He had given his all, and it had not been enough.

Hindsight made a mockery of his rescue attempt. He should have thought up a distraction, maybe by setting the grass ablaze, or stampeding the horses. Anything to keep Dugan's band busy while he freed the captives.

Time weighted by millstones crawled past. Idly, Davy observed an omen of impending dawn; the sky changed from stark black to royal blue. Grey streaks appeared. Soon the cutthroats would be roused from sleep, and within an hour they would be on the march.

Sitting up, Davy saw the north sentry stamping back and forth to ward off the morning chill. Davy blinked— and the sentry was nowhere to be seen. Perplexed, he scoured the vicinity. Other than the two men near the tongue, who had their backs to the prairie, no one else was around.

Where had the sentry gone? Davy wondered. A splash of red in the low grass gave him a clue. Beyond, shadowy specters flitted toward the encampment, converging from all different directions.

Electrified, Davy dashed to the rear, prodding Heather, Becky, and Hamlin as he passed them. "Get set. Our string of luck hasn't quite run out."

"How's that?" Heather said.

Flavius had been dozing. But something in his friend's tone sliced through his fatigue like a hot knife through wax. He rubbed the sleep from his eyes.

166

All hell broke loose.

From every quarter rose wavering war whoops, hoarse shrieks, and fierce exultation. The tumult was punctuated by yells and curses and a random smattering of shots.

"To the horses!" Davy declared, yanking the blanket wide. "Don't drag your heels or you'll be pushing up grass come spring." He forked a leg over the gate. "I'll go first."

Dropping, Davy alighted like a cat to find he had landed in the midst of bedlam. Into the camp streamed a fiery horde of painted warriors. Arrows buzzed like a swarm of bees. Lances and war clubs were being wielded with deadly efficiency. As he pivoted toward the horses, one of the attackers reared in front of him.

No timid Kanzas, these. The warrior was tall, muscular, almost stately. A hooked nose and thick lips dominated a crafty face crowned by a head that had been clean shaven except for a thin strip of spiked hair down the center, the hair held in place by a bone roach. The warrior's face, shoulders, and chest had been splashed with red pigment. In his right hand was a war club.

Pawnees, Davy guessed, just as the man delivered a blow that would have fractured his skull, had it landed. Sidestepping, Davy drove his left fist into the Pawnee's nose. The man tottered backward, recovered, and whipped the war club overhead.

Davy heard a *thwack* and a sickly rending of flesh and bone. A slug cored the Pawnee's head from left to right. The man fell, scarlet spurting from his mouth.

Lead was flying thick and fast. The defenders had rallied, the din of their rifles and pistols eclipsing the war whoops of the Pawnee. Added to the confusion were the panicked whinnies of the terrified horses and the screams of the dying and the wounded.

167

Flavius jumped to the ground. He was scared to death, but determined not to succumb. Shutting his mind to the carnage, he offered his hand to Becky, who clambered from the wagon with the agility of a monkey. Next came Heather. Last, and slowest, was Jonathan Hamlin, who hesitated with his hands on the gate.

"*Come on!*" Flavius urged. When Hamlin did not move swiftly enough to suit him, he grabbed the man's wrists and pulled him out bodily.

Davy scooped up the fallen war club. As yet, none of the others Pawnees had shown any interest in them. The rest had their hands full with Dugan's men, a third of whom were already down, either wounded or dead.

Davy saw Rickert, on one knee, snap off a shot. The next moment three feathered shafts imbedded themselves in Rickert's chest.

A river rat met the rush of a Pawnee holding a lance with nothing but a knife. The lance sheared through the riverman's sternum and burst out his back.

"Stay close!" Davy warned. Holding Becky's hand, he hurried toward the horses, stepping over the bodies of Pawnees and cutthroats alike. One of the guards had been slit from ear to ear.

Flavius was pushing Hamlin. Heather helped out as much as she could, but whenever a gun blasted close at hand, she would flinch and duck, slowing them down. "Hurry, damn it!" Flavius railed.

To Davy, the horses seemed to be miles away. Through choking gun smoke he sped, a continuous medley of inhuman cries attesting to the ferocity of the struggle.

A Pawnee spotted them and spun to contest their flight. The man held a bow, and as he snapped a hand to his quiver for an arrow, Davy hurled the war club with all the force in his sinews. It was a lot like throwing a tomahawk, which Davy had practiced countless times. The club smashed into the warrior's face, felling him instantly.

Unarmed now, Davy pressed on. Most of the fighting swirled in the middle of the camp, where Alexander Dugan and ten to twelve men were resisting to their utmost. Fully twice that many Pawnees ringed them, unleashing shafts and thrusting with lances and knives.

Davy reached the string. Untying a mare, he hiked Becky onto its back, had her clutch its mane, and swiveled to aid Heather and Hamlin.

Flavius spied a pile of supplies nearby. "I'll be right back!" he hollered, and darted toward it.

"What the—?" Davy exclaimed. He had no time to dwell on what his friend had done. Seizing Hamlin's wrists, Davy steered him to a buttermilk horse and bent to boost Hamlin up. A *thud* above him preceded a scream of mortal anguish from Heather. Davy started to straighten and bumped his head on something.

It was an arrow. The barbed point had sliced into Jonathan Hamlin below the left shoulder blade, passed completely through him, and ruptured the flesh outward high on his torso.

"*Nooooooooooooo!*" Heather flung herself forward, holding him up and shielding him from additional shafts with her own body.

Davy whirled but did not see the Pawnee responsible. He turned to help Heather, and together they succeeded in pushing Jonathan onto the horse. But as Hamlin sat hunched over, spitting blood, a second arrow transfixed him low on his left side.

Stiffening, Jonathan Hamlin flicked glazing eyes at

the empty air. "Heather?" he cried. "Oh, Heather! I loved you so!"

Heather screeched as Hamlin toppled. She would have knelt and cradled him had Davy not grabbed her by the arms and compelled her to mount. For a long moment she resisted, wailing, "Let me go to him! Please! Please!"

Shock accomplished what strength could not. Heather succumbed, and practically swooned. Davy had no trouble shoving her up. As he untied a third animal and forked its back, Flavius rushed out of the acrid smoke bearing a bundled blanket. "Hurry!" Davy coaxed.

Flavius was going as fast as he could. Hunkering, he unwrapped the blanket, revealing the contents. "Our guns!" The day before, he had seen Benchley wrap them up, and recognized the blanket among the supplies.

Now Flavius passed Liz and the Irishman's flintlocks to Davy, then claimed Matilda and his own pistols. Their knives were gone, but Davy's tomahawk had not been taken. Flavius handed it up as well.

"Let's ride!" Davy said.

The melee had resolved into frenzied personal combat. Each cutthroat was hemmed in by two or three Pawnee. Their guns spent, the defenders resorted to knives and rifle stocks.

Rufus Benchley was on one knee, his shirt ripped, his left thigh spurting his life's blood. As Davy looked on, a Pawnee brought a war club down on the crown of Benchley's head.

Davy slapped his legs against his mount. At a trot they fled, Flavius leading Heather's horse, Becky behind her mother. They covered fifty yards. Sixty.

Slowing so the others could pass him, Davy looked

over his shoulder. The sight that met his eyes brought him to a stop.

None of the Pawnees was in pursuit. In the camp, all the defenders were down, save one.

Alexander Dugan was the sole survivor, battered and bruised but otherwise unhurt, a broken rifle clutched in both hands. For some reason, the warriors were not closing in on him. Instead, when Dugan straightened and moved toward the horses, the Pawnees parted.

Davy was flabbergasted. Were they honoring his courage? His fighting ability? Or was the uncanny power of his personality having the same effect on them that it had on everyone else?

Shifting from side to side, Dugan passed the last of the painted bronze figures. Stepping to his white stallion, he gripped the reins. A smirk spread across his face. He glanced out over the plain, saw Davy. The smirk widened.

Davy lifted Liz. He cocked the hammer as Dugan mounted. He took deliberate aim as Dugan reined the stallion around. And he fired just as Alexander Dugan was on the verge of riding out of the encampment.

The ball drilled Dugan above the left eye, catapulting him from the stallion. He tumbled, rolling twice. His body came to rest beside that of another, a lean young man whose dreams of a new life in a new land had been shattered by the cruelty Alexander Dugan spread with casual disdain.

Wheeling his mount, Davy Crockett galloped into the bright shining of a new day.